# CLUTCH PLAYER

---

KYLIE GILMORE

Cover design by Sweet 'N Spicy Designs

Published by: Extra Fancy Books

ISBN-13: 978-1-942238-15-7

*Paging the doctor for a love emergency!*

**1**

______

Jared Reynolds barreled toward danger his whole life. Today was no exception. He floored the accelerator in his Ford pickup truck, speeding toward his stepbrother Vince's house on a Saturday at eight a.m. after a text that said simply: *Clutch player, you're up. Emergency.* His brothers nicknamed him clutch player because he was the guy who came through in a difficult situation. He lived for this shit. His adrenaline was pumping through his veins, and he made the ten-minute drive across town in five minutes flat.

He jiggled the knob. Locked. He leaned on the doorbell, hoping it was nothing wrong with his sister-in-law Sophia, who was newly pregnant. He had a medical supply bag with him just in case because he was the doctor in the family. He was an orthopedic surgeon, but he could do an emergency patch before transport to the hospital. The thought of something happening to the baby had him pounding on the door.

"Come on, come on," he muttered, bouncing on the balls of his feet.

Finally, Vince Marino, his older stepbrother by five years, a bulky-with-muscles construction worker with a booming voice that took shit from no one, opened the door, took one look at him and said, "Do you have a peppermint candy?"

Jared burst past him and into the living room, where he

looked around wildly for the emergency. "Where is she? Upstairs?" He was already halfway up the stairs when Vince called him back.

"She's in the bathroom off the kitchen."

He turned and raced back to the small bathroom, stopping short at the closed door. "Sophia, it's Jared. Can I come in?"

He heard the distinct sound of retching.

"No!" Sophia hollered.

He turned to Vince, who was pacing in the small galley kitchen. "Is she hurt? Is there blood?"

Vince stopped pacing and gave him a pained look. "No, just a lot of barf."

The pieces clicked into place as Jared realized what he had here was nothing more than a nervous first-time father. It wasn't that Vince didn't understand pregnancy—he'd taken a crash course in it as soon as he was asked to be a godfather last year—it was just that it was happening to Sophia. Vince's big heart couldn't take watching her suffer. Jared's adrenaline slowed, making him tired and wondering what the hell he was doing here at eight a.m. on a Saturday. It was supposed to be his day off.

"Geez, Vince, I was in full-throttle mode. Don't text me it's an emergency when it's not."

Vince shoved both hands in his brown hair, making his dark brown eyes appear even larger and filled with alarm. "She's gonna starve little Vince!"

"She's seven weeks, right?" Jared asked in his confident doctor tone.

"Yeah."

"Perfectly normal. The baby's getting what it needs and Sophia's fine."

"She's not *fine!*" Vince barked. "It's like *The Exorcist* in there!"

Sophia emerged from the bathroom in pink pajamas, her olive skin blanched, her long dark brown hair up in a messy ponytail. "Thanks, Vince, it's always nice to be compared to someone possessed. Hi, Jared." He raised a hand in greeting, and she turned to Vince. "I told you I'm fine. You didn't need to call Jared. Just go."

"I'm not leaving you like this," Vince said. "Jared'll do it."

"Do what?" Jared asked.

Sophia headed for the nearby living room, and Vince trailed after her, stopping abruptly when Sophia whirled. She pointed to her forehead and then to Vince in some kind of silent communication before walking away. Vince retreated to the kitchen, where Jared stood, leaning against the counter.

"What's with the hand signals?" Jared asked.

"Hell if I know," Vince said. "It's like PMS on steroids around here."

Jared gave him a sympathetic *women, what can you do* look while working hard to tone down his *glad it's not me* vibe. Vince turned and started digging around in a cabinet while Jared waited impatiently for Vince to explain what he needed him to do. Since he was up early on his day off, he could work more on the deck he was building off the back of his house. He loved working with tools whether they were on a house, a car, or a human body.

He cocked his head at the strange sight in front of him. It appeared Vince was making tea. He watched Vince fill the teakettle, set it on the stove over a huge roaring flame, and take out tea bags.

"Ginger tea," Vince said as if that explained all of his surprising domestic skill.

"Ah, Vince?"

Vince looked over his shoulder briefly before taking a delicate teacup with pink flowers out of the cabinet along with a matching saucer. "What?"

Jared valiantly bit back every dainty princess remark that immediately came to mind, purely out of self-preservation. "What do you need me to do?"

Vince finished arranging everything he apparently needed for tea, including a small set of tongs and a tiny spoon. Jared pressed his lips tightly together. It was right on the tip of his tongue, *Princess Vince, one lump or two?* Except Vince might take that literally and give him two lumps. To the head.

But then Vince turned, and what he said next was no laughing matter. "You're going to be Captain Cuddle."

Jared put his hands up. "No."

Captain Cuddle was a porcupine from their mom's well-known picture-book series, The Huddle-Cuddles. He'd run into Vince on a Captain Cuddle visit to the pediatric hematology-oncology ward of Eastman Hospital (where Jared worked) one Saturday a few years back. Curious, he'd insisted on tagging along, and Vince let him after Jared swore never to breathe a word about it. He'd watched as Vince donned a red T-shirt with a felt C on the front, red eye mask, blue cape, and worst of all, a gray knit cap with gray yarn that stuck up all over his head for quills. It was his superhero version of the porcupine from the book. Vince had been playing the part ever since his friend's son, Jaden, was diagnosed with cancer (and had continued even after Jaden's death because the kids loved Captain Cuddle). And while Jared respected what Vince did, he had a rep to protect at the hospital. No nurse would hook up with him if they saw him in that getup. And nurses were his main source of hookups, given that he spent nearly all of his time at work.

Vince advanced on him. "Yes. I can't let the kids down and neither can you."

Jared shook his head vigorously. "I don't know the first thing about kids. I don't know what to say or—"

"Just be friendly," Vince barked. "Read the freaking picture books. Easy."

"Ask Angel." His stepbrother Angel was a school social worker. He worked with kids all the time. Jared knew his strengths—intricate surgeries that gave his patients use of their hand again, fixing up his house, making the ladies smile with satisfaction. Not only that, he lived up to his nickname, clutch player, because just like in baseball—bottom of the last inning, two outs—he'd hit the winning run. It was about performing under pressure, coming through when you were needed most. Like last year when everyone in his family was freaking out about his stepdad Vinny's cancer diagnosis, Jared had come through, *despite* his worry. He made sure

Vinny had the best doctors, had personally reviewed every test and treatment option, and made sure he had the best home healthcare. He couldn't take full credit for Vinny's recovery, it was partly his stepdad's strength, partly good medicine, but he knew he'd been the advocate his stepdad needed. Now Vinny was cancer-free. Life-or-death situations called for a clutch player. *Not* life or porcupine.

Vince grunted. "Angel's tutoring on Saturday mornings. It's good money. You know he's saving for a house."

Jared felt a pang of guilt. He and Angel were both thirty, but Jared had been able to buy his house at twenty-four when he'd inherited a large sum of money from his biological father. Angel had been scrimping and saving for years on a social worker's salary. He tried to think of another brother who could fill in. There had to be at least one of his five brothers who could relate to kids.

"What about Gabe?" Jared asked. His oldest brother, Gabe, had a ten-month-old son, Miles. That automatically made him the better choice.

Vince jabbed him in the chest. "No one else is finding out about this gig. You're the only one who knows. You think I want to open myself up to that kind of ridicule at Sunday dinner?"

Before Jared could suggest Vince continue doing it himself, Sophia raced by, hand over her mouth, and rushed into the bathroom. The sounds of retching were unmistakable.

Vince raised a brow. "See? I'm the daddy and my job starts now. Wait here." He stalked out of the room.

Jared considered escape, but he knew Vince would hunt him down. He only lived ten minutes away in the same town of Eastman. Vince returned with a large duffel bag that Jared assumed held the costume and a stack of Huddle-Cuddle books.

Jared made one last-ditch effort. "I'm really not the right guy for this job." He was too cool to be a porcupine.

Vince set the books on the counter and shoved the bag into Jared's hands. "What're you so afraid of? You jump out of airplanes on a regular basis. These are sick kids stuck in bed."

"Skydiving is nothing like being a por—"

"Just do it," Vince snarled, all in his face.

Jared stared into those fierce dark brown eyes and considered again how to pass the buck.

"You don't have to baby me," Sophia announced as she returned to the kitchen.

Jared gestured to Sophia. "She said it. You don't have to baby her."

The teakettle whistled, which got Vince out of his face as he turned to tend to the tea. A few moments later, the scent of ginger filled the tiny kitchen.

"This'll help with the nausea," Vince told Sophia.

She raced back to the bathroom.

Vince raised a brow at Jared. "See?"

"Perfectly healthy," Jared pronounced.

Vince narrowed his eyes into slits of older-brother menace, a classic intimidation move that really worked.

Sophia returned a moment later. "False alarm. Vince, please, he obviously doesn't want to do it. Not everyone can do what you do. Stop babying me and do what you do best. Make those kids' day."

"Smart woman," Jared chimed in.

"I'm not babying you!" Vince boomed. "I'm babying the baby. Someone has to make sure little Vince doesn't starve!"

Sophia bit her lip, her eyes shiny with unshed tears that promised a lot of flowers, chocolate, and maybe jewelry would soon be in order.

"Now go sit down and sip your ginger tea!" Vince barked, not seeming to notice the shiny eyes. He turned to Jared. "Go! Ask for the nurse Emily Maguire. She'll show you what to do."

Sophia spoke in a quavery voice. "I told you I dreamed it's going to be a girl. Are you still going to love a girl?"

"Course I will," Vince replied. "I'll treat her just the same." He jabbed a finger in the air and smiled. "She'll be the first female quarterback in the NFL!"

Sophia wailed and ran out of the room. Jared winced.

Vince turned to him, his brows scrunched together like they had to confer on this confusing situation. "Now what'd I say?"

Jared picked up the duffel bag and stack of books from the counter. Vince had his hands full at home, that was for sure. "Fine, I'll do it. *One time.*"

Emily Maguire stood outside of her patient's room, blinking back tears. Ten-year-old Chris Messina had just returned with his third recurrence of cancer. The doctors were not optimistic. She swallowed over the lump in her throat. As a pediatric oncology nurse, she knew not all of her patients would survive, yet she couldn't help getting attached. She'd lost Jaden two years ago shortly after he went into the pediatric intensive care unit (PICU). She'd been away at her sister's wedding when he'd landed in PICU and hadn't taken any time off since then. Her patients needed her too much for that.

Chris's dad, Tony, had just left to get some of Chris's things from home, and she'd promised to call immediately if he took a turn for the worse. She gave herself a few moments of silent grieving for Chris's poor prognosis before taking a deep breath and heading to the nurses' station to get the goody bag ready for Vince's Captain Cuddle visit. She had to be strong for her patients' sake. Captain Cuddle was the bright spot in the children's week, which made it the bright spot in hers too. She added some pumpkin squishy balls and Halloween finger puppets to the bag since tomorrow was Halloween. A deep, unfamiliar voice rumbled behind her.

"Where can I find Emily Maguire?"

She turned and immediately became suspicious. Who was this imposter? He was dressed in the Captain Cuddle outfit she'd made, but this man wasn't as tall as Vince or as bulky, and he had light brown hair sticking out of the bottom of the cap, fair skin, and green eyes. Vince was a dark-haired, dark-eyed Italian man. "I'm Emily. Where's Vince?"

The man stepped closer and spoke near her ear, his breath hot against her skin, bringing a jolt of awareness to her long-dormant libido. "He asked me to step in today."

She met his gorgeous green eyes through the red eye mask and her throat went dry. She reminded herself to think of the children, not the fact that she was way overdue to get back on the horse, so to speak, and no horses had given her the slightest giddyup in her…pulse in a very long time. She swallowed and worked on sounding authoritative. "I still don't know who you are. You could be a thief or—"

"Gimme a break! You think any self-respecting thief would show up in this outfit?" He lowered his voice and looked around. A few other nurses looked over curiously. "Can we just get this over with?"

"Not until I know who you are. I may have to call security." She grabbed the phone on the nearby desk. His hand closed over hers, warm and strong. She ignored the electric sensation traveling up her arm at his touch. The sudden hot flash and thrumming pulse were a little harder to ignore. Geez, it had been way too long if Captain Cuddle was turning her on. The man was dressed like a porcupine, for crying out loud!

He pushed the mask up to his forehead. "I'm Jared Reynolds. I work orthopedics upstairs. Vince is my step-brother."

She slid her hand out of his grip. "Oh…I've heard of you, Dr. Reynolds." He had quite a reputation among the nurses. Now that she knew who he was, she cooled considerably. She was done with players.

"Call me Jared." He winked. "So…what'd you hear?"

She pursed her lips. They called him "Dr. One-And-Done." Everyone knew he hooked up with someone once, never to be heard from again. Still the female nurses flocked to him because the other thing they said was that it was worth it. Hmph. If they could see him now, looking boastful while wearing a gray knit cap with "quills" sticking up all over the place, they wouldn't be flocking to him. He looked absurd. She worked hard to remember that absurdity as she took in his broad shoulders tapering into a trim waist and muscular legs encased in faded jeans. She forced her gaze back to his eyes that held a glint of amusement as if he knew she'd been checking him out. His rep and cockiness reminded her she needed a man like this like she needed a hole in her heart. Been there, done that, still recovering, thank you very much.

He flashed a smile that made dimples appear in his stubbled cheeks. "Is it my surgical skills or…something else?"

She felt herself flush. "Something else," she replied primly, and when he smiled even wider, she added, "Nothing good."

He raised a brow. "Really? I've never had any complaints."

That wasn't surprising. He didn't stick around long enough to hear any. She pushed that uncharitable thought down. The important thing was the kids. Then a thought occurred to her. "Is Vince okay?"

She'd had the privilege of working with Vince Marino for the past two years as his alter ego, Captain Cuddle, and he was fabulous. So generous, so big-hearted, so sweet.

Dr. Reynolds, err, Jared, pushed his eye mask back down in place and set his mouth in a flat line. "Vince is fine. He's acting like an overprotective nut because of Sophia's morning sickness. I told him it was perfectly normal."

"Aww, he's so sweet. He's going to make a great dad."

Jared huffed. "Yeah, sweet. Alright, where do I start?"

She eyed him. "Do you have any experience with kids?"

"Sure, I have a nephew, Miles."

She frowned. "He's just a baby. Vince talks about his godson all the time. It's different with older kids." She handed him the goody bag. "Okay, start with Chris's room. He's the sickest on the ward. You want to go to the kids likely to fall asleep early first. Speak to them in a cheerful tone, read a story, and offer them a prize from the goody bag. Think you can handle all that?"

"I'm on it," he said, striding forward. He stopped abruptly. "Which room is Chris's?"

"Eighty-two."

He nodded and headed over. She followed behind him quietly and leaned near the door to hear how his first visit went.

"Hey," Jared said. "What do you think of the Sox's chances?" His tone wasn't cheerful like she'd instructed, but more casual like he was chatting with someone in the elevator.

She closed her eyes and stifled a groan. But then she heard Chris's soft voice answer, "The season is over."

"Well, we shouldn't give up hope yet," Jared replied firmly. "There's always next year."

Her throat tightened, wondering if Chris would make it to next year, while at the same time appreciating Jared's underlying message, *Hang on, kid.*

Chris spoke up. "Hey! You have green eyes. Captain Cuddle has brown eyes."

"I'm his stepbrother Captain Huddle. He asked me to visit today because he had to take care of Mrs. Cuddle. She wasn't feeling very well."

"Oh," Chris said softly. "But there's a C on your shirt! Huddle starts with an H."

"The C stands for captain. I'm gonna read you *The Huddle-Cuddle School Smashup.* This one was always my favorite because of the playground brawl."

"Was it bloody?" Chris asked eagerly.

"Oh yeah," Jared enthused.

"Cool!" Chris exclaimed.

She shook her head with a smile. That wasn't true, she knew, but it seemed Jared was quick to pick up on kids' cues to what they were secretly hoping for. Maybe he would do okay as a onetime stand-in for Vince.

Jared finished his three-hour shift as what he'd now renamed himself, Captain Huddle, and leaned against the high half wall of the nurses' station, completely exhausted. Even sick in bed, kids were a lot of work. They always wanted more stories, had an endless supply of questions, and took forever to pick prizes. He'd resorted to giving each kid a handful of prizes before moving on. And he had to admit it was damn difficult to see kids looking so sick and not be able to help them. He was a doctor who couldn't heal—the absolute worst. His own patients were mostly healthy adults with joint problems or injuries. It took a special kind of person to work day in, day out with terminally ill kids. He had to give Vince some credit too for volunteering to do this every Saturday for the past two years.

He spotted Emily walking down the hallway and followed her, taking a moment to appreciate the rear view as her hips swayed and her long, glossy brown hair swung a little back and forth when she walked. Even in plain blue scrubs he could tell she had a killer bod. He was kind of an expert at the what's-hiding-under-those-scrubs game. Her face was beautiful when she wasn't scowling at him—kind of a heart shape with smooth skin and a hint of pink to her cheeks, a cute upturned nose, and sweet pink lips. This was definitely a nurse he wanted to get to know better. He hadn't missed the chemistry between them that made her flush pink, or the fact that she'd checked him out, though she tried to hide her interest with some snappy comebacks.

"Hey, Emily," he called.

She turned, and for a moment it looked like she was going to smile at him, but just as quickly it passed and she regarded him seriously. "What?"

He pushed the eye mask to the top of his head and caught up to her. "Here," he said, handing her the empty goody bag. "The rugrats took every last prize."

Her brown eyes widened. "That was supposed to last for two weeks!"

He shrugged. "They took forever to decide, so I let them have a bunch of crap."

She scowled. "They each get one thing. I can't ask Vince to give me more and more money each time."

"Vince pays for it?"

"Yeah. The goody bag was his idea. I do the shopping and he pays."

He dug out his wallet and pulled out several twenties. "Here, sorry."

She pushed back the money. "No, I'm sorry. You didn't know. I've got it." She rubbed her forehead. "It's been a rough morning." She did look a little worn down, and now that he'd toured the ward, he could see how it could take a toll.

"Hey, you need a break? I could take you out to dinner."

Her lips twitched. "No, thank you, Captain Cuddle."

He yanked off the quill cap and eye mask. He'd nearly forgotten he was wearing it. Heat crept up his neck. Dammit. He never blushed. Still, he tried again, wanting to lift the heavy burden of her job from her shoulders, wanting to see her smile. "Drinks?"

"I'm afraid your reputation precedes you, so no," she replied, all sassy.

He grinned. "But that should make you say yes. I can be a lot of fun." He knew the nurses must speak highly of him because, after he'd scored his first few happy hookups, word got out and women chased *him* down when they wanted a good time. He always used protection, though, to ensure it was safe fun for everyone. Anyway, lately that had been getting kind of old. Seeing his older brothers settled down and insanely happy had made him start to think, with the right woman, it might be…kinda nice.

Or not. It could go the other way too—a total disaster—as he well knew.

She stared at his chest and then his bicep before yanking her gaze back to his eyes. "I'm not in the market for fun." Though he could tell she was considering it. "Tell Vince I said hi." She turned and walked away.

He deflated. It was the first time he'd gotten a *no* in so long he almost didn't know what to do with himself. "Hey, Emily," he called.

She turned. "What?"

"What kind of person doesn't like fun?"

She raised a hand above her head and pointed to herself before waving him off. She stepped into a patient's room.

"Your loss," he mumbled to himself before heading to the bathroom to change out of the costume. He didn't want to ruin the superhero illusion for the kids if they caught him transforming back to a regular guy again. He immediately felt better dressed like himself and headed out the door. He drove straight to Vince's house. At least that humiliating Captain Huddle experience was over. He'd put the whole thing behind him and pretend it never happened.

As soon as Vince opened the door, Jared handed over the costume bag.

Vince stepped back, out of reach, and the bag hit the floor. "Nope. Until we get to the second trimester, it's all you. She's gonna starve little Vince if I don't keep an eye on her."

"It's Isabella!" Sophia hollered from somewhere inside.

Vince jerked a thumb behind him. "You see what I'm dealing with here." He rolled his eyes and then hollered over his shoulder. "We don't know that until the twenty-week ultrasound!" He turned back to Jared. "I know more than her on account of my godfather preparation." He hollered over his shoulder again. "Read the book, Soph! Then you can speak to me with knowledge." He added under his breath, "Not ignorance."

Jared ground his teeth. "How long are we talking?"

Vince shrugged. "Best-case scenario? Six, seven more weeks."

"Seven more weeks!"

"What's the big deal? The kids scare you off so fast?" He tossed the costume bag, and Jared caught it in the chest with one hand. "Don't be a wuss. You're a fucking doctor."

Jared squared his shoulders. "I know I'm a fucking doctor. Dressing like a porcupine isn't in the job description."

"Well, it should be." Vince glanced over his shoulder and then turned back to him. "I'm gonna get her some saltines and ginger ale. You got this, okay? You're my clutch player."

The nickname that normally felt like a compliment felt like a damn straitjacket now. It wasn't just the humiliating costume. It was the helpless feeling of not being able to fix the kids. He *always* fixed his patients.

"Vince, the kids—"

Vince shut the door in his face.

"Like you better," Jared grumbled to the door. Dammit. He turned back to his truck, mumbling about aggravating brothers and no-fun brunettes with sexy bods the whole way home.

## 2

___

Emily returned to her quiet one-bedroom apartment in Clover Park that afternoon and quickly changed into a sweater and jeans. She flopped down on the sofa, stretching out with a purple knitted blanket and her favorite romance author's newest release. *You'd think I'd be completely turned off by romance.* But with her job, she needed the sweet escape.

Her cell vibrated on the nearby end table, and she snatched it up. Shit. A text from Michael. Her ex-husband hadn't called, texted, or emailed in two years. *We need to talk.*

Ha! She immediately texted back. *No, we don't.*

*It's important.*

She put the cell down. Forget it. They had nothing to talk about. The papers, news stations, and gossip mags had taken care of all that. What more was there to say? Michael was a rat. She was the idiot who—

Her cell rang. She picked it up. "How did you get my number?"

"I keep tabs on you," Michael responded smoothly.

She hung up. Then she powered the phone down.

There was a knock at the door. *No. It couldn't be.*

She peeked through the peephole. She let out a stream of curses and wished she had a baseball bat handy. Not because she feared Michael would hurt her. Because she wanted to clobber him.

He knocked again. She sighed. He was standing there holding a bouquet of red roses. They weren't her favorite. She was partial to tulips, but Michael always apologized with red roses. There'd been a lot of red roses in her past.

"Go away," she called through the door.

"Emily, it's important. I drove an hour just to see you." She'd moved an hour south for a fresh start, away from him and everyone who knew her.

She rolled her eyes. "No one told you to come over. How did you know where I lived?"

"The Internet makes it easy to find someone."

That was probably true. She'd returned to her maiden name, but Michael knew it.

"Please just hear me out. I really need to talk to you."

She sighed. "Just a minute." He wouldn't go away. That much she knew. She shoved her feet into sneakers and stepped out into the upstairs hallway, which was open to the outdoors, shutting the door behind her. "Make it quick."

He offered her the roses, and she crossed her arms, refusing to accept them. He looked the same—dark brown hair cropped short, sharp brown eyes, high cheekbones, a strong jaw. He'd modeled a bit in college. His looks played well in the press. Even now, on a Saturday, he'd dressed as if he might be caught on camera with a crisp light blue pin-striped button-down shirt, navy blue pants, and designer light brown dress shoes.

"I still love you," he said in a voice meant to sound earnest, but it came off insincere to her ears. She wasn't fooled for one minute. He wanted something.

"I don't love you back. Is that all?"

He paced for a moment and stopped. "We had it good. In the beginning. Nothing could stop us."

She merely gave him a look that said *so?* She'd been twenty-five to Michael's sophisticated thirty when she'd met him at one of her parents' pool parties, the kind where the country club set stood *around* the pool, sipping white wine in their summer whites, and no one ever took a swim. He was new in town, and her parents were thrilled to introduce her to the wealthy lawyer with political aspirations. Her romantic heart had been taken in by his charm and dashing good looks, as well as the over-the-top courtship full of flowers, jewelry, and extravagant dinners. In hindsight, it was clear he'd been on the hunt for a wife for political reasons, as just another component of his campaign for state attorney general. After a whirlwind three-month romance and a fairy-tale wedding, they had one good year of marriage followed by two years of Michael cheating and apologizing.

At first she'd been slow on the uptake. Just some suspicions. When she'd told him her concerns, he made her feel like she was crazy for even thinking them. But then she had proof: another woman named Emily texting him with sexy invitations. What followed still made her shudder. She'd gone down that depressing path too many times to let herself fall headlong into the spiral of shame.

Michael raised his palms. "With you I won the state attorney general office. Voters loved us together."

"And then they didn't."

Michael stepped closer, his voice dripping sincerity. "I'm running for public office again. State senator, a stepping-stone to the national level. The campaign starts next week right after election day. We've already got a campaign committee. We're getting ready to announce my intention and build from there."

"So what do you need me for?"

"A public reconciliation—"

"No." She turned to go, and he grabbed her by the elbow. "Hands off!" she shouted. He dropped his hand. She took a deep breath and turned back to him. "I will never *ever* go back to you."

"It would be different this time. I'd be faithful. We could have the children you always wanted. With you by my side, it will restore your name in the public eye. They won't associate you with that—" at her narrowed eyes, he finished lamely "— other news story."

She hated the way her name had been dragged through the mud as if she was as dirty as he was. Hated all the cameras, the microphones shoved in her face, the news vans camped out in front of their house. She closed her eyes as the shame and humiliation washed over her again.

"If you forgive me," Michael said earnestly, "the voters will forgive me. And we'll both benefit."

She hadn't forgiven him. She didn't think she ever would. He hadn't just cheated, hadn't just lied to her face over and over, he'd betrayed her in the most humiliating, public way possible.

"Don't contact me again," she said firmly. "I don't forgive you, and I never will."

With that, she turned, went inside her apartment, and locked the door behind her. She didn't hear him walking away. Needing even more space, she retreated to her bedroom and locked that door too. She flopped on the queen-size brass bed, rolled over, and stared at the ceiling, her eyes surprisingly dry. *Guess I'm all out of tears for Michael.*

But then she thought about the children she'd always wanted, and her eyes filled. Because, at thirty, being married again with a child of her own seemed impossibly out of reach. She never met the right kind of man. The kind with eyes (and heart) only for her. Maybe he didn't exist. Maybe she was clinging to a romantic fantasy.

She threw an arm over her stinging eyes. She had children, in a way. Sick children who needed her. And, though it hurt her heart when she lost one of them, it only strengthened her resolve to pour everything she had into keeping the others comfortable and alive. That was what gave meaning to her life.

Her very safe life focused on work, cooking, and reading.

Dammit. What happened to the old Emily? The one who was happy and open to new experiences, new relationships. She used to be more fun loving, loved meeting new people. Hell, she'd backpacked all over Europe after college having tons of adventures like bike riding through Provence and hitchhiking through Italy. She'd made pilgrimages to theme parks all over the country on a quest to ride every wooden roller coaster.

She leaped out of bed. Stupid Michael screwing with her head. Fuck him. It was time to start living again. She grabbed her cell and her purse and headed out the door. Thankfully Michael had left. She was going to hang out at Garner's Sports Bar & Grill. A nice drink surrounded by people would prove she was still open to new experiences. Maybe—with her friends Charlotte and Megan at her side—she'd even flirt with a handsome stranger. She called her friends. Neither of them were home but promised to meet up with her at five. That gave her a good three hours to kill. She'd walk to Main Street, a thirty-minute walk, and then hang out in the shops.

She headed to Book It, browsing all the new releases and then settling in the attached Something's Brewing Café, treating herself to a cappuccino while she people watched in the crowded space. Mostly people working on their laptops and a few couples. Finally, it was nearly five, so she headed across the street to Garner's. She took a seat at the very end of the crowded dark cherrywood bar and texted Charlotte and Megan, letting them know where she was sitting. The dining area to the right was filling up already for dinner.

The bartender, Josh, arrived. He was thirtyish with dark brown hair that curled a bit; his brown eyes were warm, his smile infectious. She beamed at him, appreciating the fact that he was always friendly and flirty, yet never crossed the line into uncomfortable pickup territory. His cheerful demeanor earned him lots of tips, especially from the women. She ordered herself a Cosmopolitan because it sounded like she was about to take a fun, exotic trip.

"You got it, gorgeous," he said in his deep baritone voice.

She glanced around the bar and jolted when she glimpsed Dr. Reynolds sitting at the opposite end of the bar. The man sitting next to him had to be his brother. Same light brown hair, same gorgeous cheekbones. They were watching a football game on the TV mounted in one corner of the bar. She briefly considered bolting. The last thing she needed today was another run-in with a player. But then she remembered she was tired of being that Emily, hiding in her hurting little shell. It was time to take a baby step out there. To find the old fun-loving Emily again and join the living. She would not bolt.

Her drink arrived, and she took a sip and then another. Then she grabbed her drink, hopped off the bar stool, and casually walked around the other side of the bar, stopping next to Jared and his brother. Their backs were to her.

She tapped Jared's shoulder. He glanced over his shoulder and then did a double take. "Emily! What're you doing here?"

She lifted one shoulder. "Same as you, I guess."

"You live in town?"

"Yup."

He flashed a dimpled smile, and she found herself smiling back. "I grew up here. You live in town long?"

"Just two years."

They stared at each other for a long moment. The warmth in his green eyes held her momentarily in thrall, like she was the most wonderful woman he'd ever clapped eyes on. His brother cleared his throat, breaking the spell. She tried to focus on his brother, who was regarding her curiously, but all she could think was that she now understood why women flocked to Jared. He probably looked at everyone like that.

"Oh," Jared said, "this is my brother Gabe." She *knew* it had to be his brother. And then Gabe smiled, revealing a dimple in his stubbled cheek, making the resemblance even closer.

Gabe offered his hand, and she shook it. "Nice to meet you."

"You too," she said.

"So, you want to sit with us?" Jared asked.

She hesitated, tempted to linger, but then quickly decided she wasn't ready for the likes of a player like Jared. Baby steps.

"No, I'm meeting some friends," she said breezily. "Just wanted to say hi."

Jared's brows scrunched down. "O-kay."

"Hi." She wiggled her fingers, smiled, and returned to her

seat. She congratulated herself on being forward and friendly instead of her usual closed-off protective ways.

Ten minutes later, she found herself fidgeting on her bar stool, debating what to do. Jared kept looking at her, but every time she caught him looking, he'd turn away. It was incredibly…awkward. But also kind of flattering. She wondered if he'd come over to her, but he didn't. Just kept drinking, talking to his brother, and sneaking looks her way. She smiled a little. She couldn't remember the last time she felt that butterfly fluttering in her stomach or quiet excitement just from a look across the room. It was good. Just enough for her.

She'd probably never see him again unless she made a big effort to find out his schedule at the hospital and meet him in the hospital cafeteria on breaks. Ha! Like she'd ever make an effort for any man. She was so over that. From here on out, she'd keep things fun and flirty and light. Why risk the heartbreak? She sipped her drink and peeked over at Jared again. He looked away in a hurry. She giggled to herself.

*Uh-oh.* He was coming over. She smoothed her hair and swallowed. *Okay, calm down. No big deal. Just be fun and flirty and light.*

"What's so funny over here?" Jared asked with a smile that made laugh lines form around his sparkling green eyes and dimples appear in his cheeks. Not that she was noticing every little detail about him.

"You keep looking at me," she answered honestly.

"And that's funny to you?"

She nodded and took a sip of her drink.

He set his beer down and leaned an elbow on the bar, close enough to make her extremely aware of his size, a good head taller than her, and muscular build. He smelled like clean soap, warm apple pie, and spice. "Why wouldn't you sit with us? You're just here by yourself."

"I told you I'm meeting friends."

"Are they invisible?"

She choked on a laugh. "No."

His green eyes gazed into hers. "That smile just made my night."

She held up a hand. "Stop."

He held up his hand and pressed it against her raised hand, bringing a surprising jolt of heat. "Stop what?"

She dropped her hand. "Don't do your little pickup routine on me. It won't work."

He leaned down to her ear, the words hot against her skin. "And why is that?"

She met his green eyes very bravely considering she was already feeling overheated from his proximity. "Because I'm immune to players and their player ways."

"Good thing I'm not a player, then." He tucked a lock of her hair behind her ear.

She untucked her hair and tossed it over her shoulder. "You are Dr. One-and-Done. Don't think I don't know what that means."

He gave her a slow, sexy smile. "One what?"

She took a sip of her drink, ignoring him.

He tugged her hair playfully. "One what?"

She gave him a sideways glance. "You know."

"Are we talking about the big O?"

She flushed and bit back a smile. "You're terrible."

"Some people don't even get the one, so, ya know—" he raised his brows "—seems like a good thing to me."

She shook her head. "Bragging player ways."

One corner of his mouth lifted. "It's good to have someone really sensible like yourself to put me in my place."

She raised her glass. "You're welcome."

He picked up his glass and tapped it against hers. "You want to grab a bite?"

She took another sip of her drink. "It's girls' night. They'll be here soon."

"Another time? I don't spend enough time with sensible women."

She laughed. "Oh, really? What kind of women do you spend time with?"

He pulled a serious face. "I spend time with a lot of clowns."

She burst out laughing and put a hand on his arm. "You do not!"

He looked down at her hand still on his arm, and she dropped it. "Save me from the clowns. I'm begging you. The rubber noses, the big feet—" he shuddered "—you don't want to know what's under the striped rompers." He grinned, looking way too irresistible. "You gonna help me out?"

Fun and flirty, she reminded herself. That was truly all she could handle right now. "I'm too sensible to say yes," she told him with a smile.

He stiffened. "Suit yourself."

Guess he was done flirting. She returned to her drink. "I will."

He stalked off. This time he didn't look her way at all. She wasn't disappointed, she told herself. It was just a harmless flirtation. And then Charlotte arrived, all big hugs and hand gestures, asking about her day. She told her about Michael's visit and forgot all about Jared.

She didn't notice him leaving with a last long look sent her way.

Didn't notice the way he strode out the door either, his cute ass in faded jeans giving her a nice view.

And she really didn't notice the way he seemed to take all the excitement of the evening with him.

**3**

---

Jared was alone in the hospital break room on Wednesday before his afternoon surgery when the news on the wall-mounted TV caught his eye. Was that Emily? He stepped closer. It really looked like her. The TV had been muted, but the headline said "Michael Spitz sex scandal may hurt run for Senate." Emily seemed to be rushing away from reporters in a series of video clips. He looked around for the remote and finally got sound just as the report was ending, catching the reporter saying, "The former state attorney general hopes the voters can forgive him as his wife, Emily, has. He'll be running for senate with her by his side."

Jared's jaw dropped. Emily was married? Sex scandal? What the hell!

The reporter went on. "Emily Spitz couldn't be reached for comment, and their reconciliation remains unconfirmed."

He'd been thinking about her ever since he ran into her at Garner's on Saturday. It wasn't just that she was beautiful. It was the way she kept sneaking looks at him. He could've sworn she was interested, but then she'd shut him down again. He didn't want to be drawn to someone not interested in him, but he was. Even more so after he'd asked around at work about her on Monday. Her reputation at the hospital was fantastic. She went above and beyond her job description

—coordinating therapy-dog visits, costumed-character visits, and art therapy for the kids. All programs the hospital didn't have funding for until she started applying for grants and getting local organizations involved. He admired that kind of dedication to her patients.

She was the real deal—beautiful, sexy, smart, kind, great with kids. No question she'd be a great mom. Whoa. Where had that come from? It must be his older brothers rubbing off on him, with Gabe being a dad now, Vince's wife pregnant, and his older stepbrother, Nico, recently married and making noises about having a large family of his own. Even the ultimate bachelor, his older brother Luke, had just gotten engaged. His sisters-in-law were great too. Kinda got Jared thinking…bah, it didn't matter anyway. Emily was married.

At least now he knew why she rejected him. He remembered that weasel Michael Spitz a few years back. He'd been caught soliciting not one but three different prostitutes, and he called them all "Emily" after his wife. Sick bastard. Emily Maguire was Emily Spitz. He was having trouble wrapping his mind around the fact that Emily had forgiven her husband and was supporting his run for senate. Was she a glutton for punishment? Was that why she was drinking alone on Saturday before her friends arrived? What woman in her right mind would stand by their husband after all that? It couldn't possibly be true.

That night Jared found himself settling on the sofa with a beer and his laptop to look up more on the Emily Spitz story. Damn. She'd been everywhere. He hadn't realized how big the scandal had been. All over the news and gossip rags. The Internet had been on fire over it. In all the photos she looked the picture of a tragic victim, always distraught, always on the run. Her husband looked contrite and remorseful. He couldn't fathom why she'd ever want to go back to that life. Maybe some part of her still loved him. He knew how hard it was to get over someone. He took a long swallow of beer. It'd taken him a long time to get over Jen. He'd kept things light and casual with the ladies ever since she'd dumped him after six months of living together (and a year of dating before that). Turned out he wasn't as exciting as she'd thought. Humph.

He set his beer and laptop on the table and stood, suddenly needing to pound something with a hammer. Of course, he and Jen hadn't been married, only lived together. She'd dumped him shortly after he'd finished his residency at the hospital a year ago, saying she'd been "disappointed" with their relationship. Apparently, after all the fun dates he took her on to amusement parks for the crazy coasters and parasailing and skydiving, she accused him of turning into a homebody.

He headed for his woodworking tools in the garage since it was too dark to hammer the half-finished deck. He was still plenty exciting, was still an adrenaline junkie, but he was also an orthopedic surgeon. It was a demanding, sometimes stressful job. He had to be perfect in the operating room, couldn't make any mistakes that might cause harm or necessitate a second surgery, or God forbid, lose a patient. He was always conscious of the need for accuracy with the often delicate surgeries needed for his specialty on hands. He worked on other parts of the body too—hips and knees mostly—but he was the go-to guy with hands. And he'd found working on projects around the house helped him unwind. He needed that more than an adrenaline rush, though he still made time for the occasional adventure. And plenty of hookups. So what if he always invited women back to his place? That didn't make him a homebody. He had a nice four-bedroom Colonial conveniently located only blocks from the hospital.

He headed for the nearly finished five-shelf maple bookcase in the garage, put on gloves and safety goggles, and powered up the sander, pushing all thoughts of Jen from his mind. He got in the zone as he sanded and smoothed. He felt another pang of sympathy for Emily with all that her husband had dragged her through. He had to check in with her and make sure she knew she deserved better than the likes of Michael Spitz.

~

By her Saturday morning shift, Emily was downright fraz-zled. She'd told Michael in no uncertain terms that she would not be getting back together with him, yet he'd publicly included her in his political announcement on Wednesday as if she were. She'd been dodging phone calls from the press ever since. How dare he drag her into this! She knew exactly what he was up to. It didn't matter if the rumors of their reconciliation were true, it was news and that put him in the spotlight again. All of those awful pictures and news clips of her in total humiliation were on TV again. And what did he care? By the time the press realized she wasn't actually giving him a second chance, he'd be onto his next bid for attention.

She pressed her fingers to her temples and closed her eyes. She'd hardly slept at all since the news broke. She could barely eat. Dammit. This could not be happening again.

"Hey, Emily."

She looked up and met the green eyes of the imposter Captain Cuddle. Jared again. Just what she needed when she was on the verge of a major meltdown. He'd better not come on to her. She was ready to kick someone's ass. Or cry in the corner. It could go either way.

"Where's Vince?" she asked.

"I'm on cuddle duty for the next six or seven weeks," he said glumly.

"Is Sophia in that bad of shape?"

"Vince thinks so." He leaned close and she breathed in his clean warm scent. "Between you and me, he's totally babying her. She's fine."

"That sounds like Vince."

"I saw you on the news—"

"Don't."

He cocked his head, making the porcupine quills bounce. "Don't what?"

"Don't go there. I just want to get through my shift without being reminded of it and go home."

He gave her a long look that was made less serious by the porcupine hat, red eye mask, giant C on his chest, and blue cape.

She bit back a smile and handed him the goody bag. "Go do your thing, Captain Cuddle."

He snagged the bag. "It's Captain *Huddle*, thank you very much. Me and my Reynolds brothers, Gabe and Luke, were the Huddle hedgehogs in the books. The Marinos were the Cuddle porcupines."

"Oh, really?" She found herself smiling for the first time in days. "I stand corrected. You could easily pass for a hedgehog."

He lifted his nose. "Hedgehogs have a pointier nose."

"I could sew you a pointy pink nose."

"No, thank you," he said with grave seriousness.

She laughed.

"You deserve better than Michael Spitz," he said, and before she could say she wasn't with him, he whirled away, his blue cape flying out behind him as he strode toward Chris's room.

She shook her head, bemused by the unexpected compliment, and went back to work. She typically worked the seven a.m. to one p.m. shift on Saturdays. As it got closer to noon, she decided lunch and a nap were all she could handle today after work.

One of the nurses, Carrie, a young blond woman with glasses, hurried over to her. Carrie often came to her with questions.

"Yes?" Emily asked with a smile.

"A bunch of news vans are in the parking lot," Carrie whispered. "The other nurses are saying it's for you."

Emily looked around, and the nurses nearby turned their heads away. She blew out a breath. She'd moved away to start fresh, but everything followed her thanks to Michael. "Okay. Thanks for letting me know, Carrie."

She headed to the small break room and peered out the window to the parking lot. Three news vans and reporters stood by the entrance of the hospital, cameras and microphones at the ready. She broke into a sweat. Shit. She was not prepared for this. Especially not with the level of exhaustion she felt from her insomnia. The shame and humiliation felt fresh. She felt like an utter fool for being the goody-goody wife who stood by him for far too long.

Anger flared in her again. How dare he make her feel this way! She refused to get caught up in this shit again. She'd wait the press out. She'd have lunch in the hospital cafeteria, and then help the other nurses where needed until the press lost interest. It must be a slow news week. Any minute some fire or explosion or bizarre event would pull them to a more interesting story.

She stepped back into the ward and went to the nurses' station. "It's not true, you know," she told the three nurses standing there, including her supervisor, Jane. "I'm not going back to him. He's using me for his own political gain."

"Don't worry about it," Jane, a kindly middle-aged woman with short brown hair, said. "What you do in your personal life isn't our concern."

"I'm not doing anything," Emily insisted. "That's just a lie to get him more press."

Jared appeared at her side and handed back the goody bag. "I saw the news vans."

She felt like she was going to scream. "Excuse me, I need to…be someplace."

She walked away. Jared appeared at her side again, eye mask pushed up to the top of his head. "I can help you."

She stopped. "Help me what?"

"Help you get out of the building undetected and avoid the news vans."

She narrowed her eyes. "How?"

He inclined his head toward the exit. "Follow me."

"Where?"

"To the supply closet upstairs."

"Excuse me, but I don't go into supply closets with strange men."

He shook his head with a smile. "You're awfully suspicious. And I'm not a strange man. You know where I work, you know my stepbrother, you know me as a loveable hedgehog. How much better could you know me?"

"A lot more!"

He grinned, and adorable dimples formed in his cheeks.

She looked away. "I didn't mean it like that!"

"Come on." He leaned down and spoke directly in her ear. "We'll change you into Captain Huddle in the supply closet and go out the service exit in the back."

She thought about that. It might work. "My shift's not over."

"I'll wait."

She knew she wasn't as focused on work as she should be and quickly decided to ask Jane if she could leave early. "Give me a minute."

She went back to Jane, who shooed her out. She returned to Jared's side, and he started walking quickly toward the exit by the stairs. Most people took the other exit by the elevators. He opened the door to the stairwell and walked briskly up three flights of stairs. She followed behind, a little out of breath at his breakneck pace. His legs were longer.

He inclined his head to follow him and she did, stepping around the corner and into a supply closet. He turned on the light, locked the door, and turned to her. "Ready?"

The space was small, forcing them to stand close enough that she could feel his body heat. Or maybe she was just over-heated from…the trip upstairs. "I guess so."

He plopped the porcupine hat on her head. Then he handed her the eye mask.

"How'd you know about the service exit?" she asked. "That's just supposed to be for suppliers."

He flashed a smile. "Or for nurses who don't want to be seen leaving the building with me."

She set the eye mask and hat on a nearby shelf. "Do you sneak out nurses a lot through the service exit?"

He untied the cape and set it on the shelf with the mask and hat. "Lucky for you, I do. But, in my defense, *they* hunt *me* down." He winked. "I'm both fun and discreet."

She rolled her eyes. "Shirt."

He took a small step back to take the T-shirt off over his gray long-sleeved shirt, giving her a glimpse of golden skin and mouthwatering abs. She quickly looked away. He pushed the warm shirt into her hand.

"Turn around," she told him.

"Why? You naked under your scrub shirt?"

He lifted the end of the shirt to peek, and she slapped his hand away. "Jared!"

"What? You've got some kind of undershirt on."

"It's a tank top. Would you just turn around?" She didn't want her tank top to pull up with her scrub shirt.

He turned. "Okay, but I have to warn you, I have eyes in the back of my head."

She found herself smiling despite the stressful situation. "I thought that was just moms that had that." She pulled off her scrubs shirt and set it on the nearby shelf.

"So do horny doctors. No one ever told you that?"

"No!" she said on a laugh. She pulled the T-shirt over her tank top. It was warm and smelled like soap, apple pie, and Jared. How long had it been since she'd worn a man's shirt? A vision of wearing her ex-boyfriend's T-shirt came to her vividly. Another heartbreaker for an altogether different reason. She was extremely unlucky in the love department.

"Okay," she said over the lump in her throat.

He turned back. "What's wrong?"

She was taken aback, surprised he knew she was upset. "Nothing."

He tilted his head and studied her. "You sure? Nothing more than you're in a supply closet hiding from the press in a porcupine costume with a horny doctor?"

She laughed and he grinned, laugh lines forming around his green eyes. "Nope. Nothing more than that."

He slid the eye mask on her, settled the hat over her head, and tied the cape around her shoulders expertly. Somehow him dressing her in the small space felt intimate.

He gazed at her for a moment, his warm hands resting on her shoulders. "You look adorable. You should've been Captain Huddle all along."

She shook her head. "The kids know me. Besides, it's nice,

especially for the boys, to have some male energy in the wing. Usually it's a lot of women nurses taking care of them."

He slid his hands from her shoulders down her arms, leaving a tingling path before stopping to squeeze both of her hands. "You like male energy?"

Her breath caught at the heated look in his eyes. "We should go," she said in what she hoped was a convincing voice because she was getting a little too cozy in the supply closet with Dr. One-and-Done.

He nodded once and pulled her quickly out of the space, still holding her hand. They hurried down the hall, up another flight of stairs, and down a service elevator. Her heart raced as the elevator descended to the main floor. She really, really hoped this worked. Jared, at her side, was utterly calm. The elevator doors opened into a dingy back hallway. Jared went ahead of her, opened the exit door, and she followed, stepping out into bright sunshine and an empty blacktopped area.

She stopped and realized she hadn't thought this through. The parking lot was on the other side of the building. They'd still have to walk around to get to her car or his. "Now what?"

"Now we walk away."

He took her hand and started walking toward the service driveway and then onto a side street. She stopped, but he pulled her along. "Come on," he said. "I live a few blocks from here."

"Wait, we're going to your house?"

"Sure. We'll have lunch and hang out. Then we'll call over to the hospital, and when the coast is clear, you can pick up your car."

"Oh." She hadn't realized she was going to be hanging out with him at his place. He might've mentioned it. Still, his plan had worked, and she found herself relaxing more and more the further they got from the hospital.

Finally they reached a well-maintained Colonial with stained wood siding and white trim. The yard was neat with lush grass and hedgerows on either side of the small front porch.

"Welcome to Chez Reynolds, Madam Porcupine," he said grandly, opening the front door and ushering her in.

She stepped inside, simultaneously relieved that she'd actually made her escape from the press and nervous that she was now in the infamous love den of Dr. Reynolds. She looked around, expecting some cheesy bachelor pad with a huge TV and sofa, but instead the space was surprisingly homey with a honey-colored wood coffee table, matching end tables, and a five-shelf bookcase. The dark green sofa was a sectional with a chaise lounge on one end that would be perfect for stretching out when watching TV. He did have the expected large flat-screen TV mounted to the wall. A throw rug with round circles of ruby red, orange, and yellow reminded her of fall. It was exactly the kind of homey space she would've done herself.

She turned to him. "Thank you. That could've went so-o-o badly. We both could've ended up in the news like some kind of sex scandal love triangle. I appreciate you taking that risk."

He pulled the hat off her head and then the eye mask. "It was nothing." He smoothed her hair with his warm hand. "I'm the idiot always running toward danger."

She untied the cape herself before he could get a chance to undress her further. "Well, today I'm glad."

He smiled at her, his warm green eyes holding her in thrall again with that most-wonderful-woman-in-the-world gaze he did so well. "Me too."

She tore her gaze away. No man had ever looked at her like that. *Imagine what that look could do to you in bed.* Not that she was lining up for a turn.

She took a step back and gestured for him to turn around. It wasn't that she cared about him seeing her tank top. It was just the tank had a habit of clinging to her clothes as she took them off.

"Don't worry," he said, "I'll cover my eyes." He slapped a hand over his eyes and peeked at her between his fingers.

"You're shameless."

He grinned and dropped his hand. "I really am." He turned away, giving her privacy.

She pulled off the shirt and realized in her rush to escape that she'd left her scrubs shirt in the supply closet. She crossed her arms, a little chilly now in just her tank top and scrubs pants. "I left my work shirt in the supply closet."

He turned, his gaze dropping to her breasts and then snapping back to her eyes. "I'll get you a sweatshirt," he said and quickly headed upstairs.

"Thanks." She went to admire the empty bookcase. The wood was gorgeous with a beveled trim and still carried a woodsy scent. She inspected the rest of the furniture, which also had beveled trim in matching wood stain. It was all quite beautiful, like the expensive pieces you'd find in a high-end furniture store.

Jared cleared his throat, and she turned. "Did you make this furniture?"

One corner of his mouth lifted. "Yup. How did you know? Amateurish?"

"Not at all. It's gorgeous. I guessed because the bookcase smells freshly cut and it's empty." She admired it some more before turning back to him. "You're very skilled."

He handed her a red University of Medicine and Dentistry New Jersey (UMDNJ) sweatshirt probably from where he went to medical school. She quickly slipped on the oversized shirt, feeling warm and safe in it like a big fleecy hug. She lifted her long hair out of the collar.

He gazed at her for a long moment. "It's just a hobby. Relaxes me to do some woodworking. You hungry?"

And, to her surprise, her appetite was back. "Yes."

**4**

———

Jared slapped together a couple of ham and cheese sand-wiches and poured Fritos on the plates. Emily had already settled at the round table in his eat-in kitchen, sitting ramrod straight. He figured she was tense after being front-page news again. He set a plate in front of her and took the seat next to her. He dove into lunch and gave her a sideways glance to make sure she was eating too. After a few moments, he asked, "You want to tell me your side of the scandal story?" She'd never spoken about it publicly. He was really curious to know her take on it. And now that she was sitting in his kitchen, so close, so beautiful, he also really needed to know if she was married.

Emily froze, sandwich halfway to her mouth. "Can I get a drink?"

"Sure, what do you want? Water? Milk? Gatorade?"

"Any alcohol?"

"Oh, ho, ho. Hitting the hard stuff this early, are we?"

She blew out a breath. "I've had a rough week."

"I hear ya." He stood. "How you like scotch?"

"Never had it."

"Well, you are in for a treat. This is the good stuff." He poured them both a small amount in a couple of glass tumblers and set them on the table. "Bottoms up." He took a healthy swallow, feeling the burn down his throat to his stomach. "Ahh."

She did the same, swallowing the whole thing down, and then started a coughing fit that made him laugh. *Newbie.*

"You like it?" he asked.

She wiped her eyes. "Yes," she croaked. She took a bite of sandwich.

He took pity on her and got up to fetch her a glass of milk.

"I'll take another," she said.

He froze. "Really?"

"Hit me." She slammed the glass on the table.

He shook his head. "All right, but I expect some juicy secrets after two drinks."

She tried to glare at him but just ended up looking adorable with her pink pursed lips. He poured her a glass of milk, and then with his back to her, he watered down her next serving of scotch. He set them both in front of her, grabbed a glass of water for himself, and adjusted his chair a little closer to her, hoping it would lead to some good secret spilling.

She drank the whole glass of scotch in one long swallow, wiped her mouth with the back of her hand and coughed. "Thanks," she croaked.

He dipped his head. They ate their lunch in silence for a few minutes. He'd discovered that a well-timed silence could get women talking. Emily didn't disappoint.

"You know the problem with men?" she asked.

He leaned in. "Tell me."

"Big cheaters," she pronounced with a nod. She pointed a Frito at him, looked at it, and took a bite.

"That's hardly fair to paint us all with the same brush. I never cheated. I just don't stick around. So your ex was a cheater. Ex, right?"

She murmured something that sounded like *mmm-hmmm*, or it might've been a really long *mmm*. Either way, he took that as a yes.

He pounded a fist on the table. "Fuck him. He didn't deserve you."

"I'm never gonna fuck him again!"

He raised his fist for a fist bump, and she gave him one. He took a bite of sandwich and then a drink of water. "So, tell me your version of the scandal. We've all heard his side, but you refused to speak about it."

She sighed and took a bite of sandwich.

"I'll tell you one of my secrets."

That got her attention. She set her sandwich down, pushed her long dark brown hair behind her ears, and regarded him curiously. "Really?"

"Really. Only if you promise to share one of your scandal secrets."

"You first."

"Okay. I, uh, gosh, this is hard for me." He looked at the table, fighting back a grin.

She took his hand and held it. "It's okay. This won't leave this room."

"Sometimes I have impure thoughts."

She scowled and shoved his hand back on the table.

"Ouch. Be careful." He lifted his hand and wiggled his fingers. "These hands are precision instruments."

She picked up a Frito and pointed it at him. "Are you ever serious?"

"Not if I can help it."

She stared at the Frito then licked it. His jeans got tight.

"He is your ex, right?" he asked. "You're divorced?"

"Yup. Totally and completely dee-vorced." She put the Frito in her mouth and chewed. "I'm never getting married again. Men are pigs."

"Is that why you turned me down?"

"I told you why I turned you down." She fed him a Frito. "Your reputation precedes you."

He wanted her, there was no question. He couldn't resist trying one more time. "My rep is overrated," he informed her.

She raised a brow. "Yeah? They say you're one and done, but it's worth it."

He chuckled. "That's why you called me Dr. One-and-Done. Maybe it's not overrated then. That doesn't make me a pig. Everyone knows going in it's just for fun."

"Yeah, yeah. That's what they all say." She went back to her sandwich. "Tell me a real secret," she said around a mouthful of sandwich. "I really want to know about you."

No one ever asked what was in his head. Most women just liked the package, his body and what it could make them feel. He double-checked if she really wanted to know. She set her sandwich down and stared at him, her body stock-still. "Go on," she said softly.

He put his sandwich down, took a deep breath, and blurted, "I never commit because then they might figure out I'm not so great and leave me." A weight lifted from his shoulders just saying that out loud. He'd had that fear in the back of his mind ever since Jen left him.

Her brown eyes widened. "Jared, wow. That was so deep." She propped her head on her hand and stared at him. "Has that ever happened to you?"

"Yeah. Last year after I finished my residency." He ate some more sandwich, and when she just sat there, head propped on her hand, listening, he added, "We lived together for six months. She left because I wasn't exciting enough. As much as I'm an adrenaline junkie, I also like working on the house. You know, fixing things, making stuff. Sometimes I'll work on the truck. I always find something to do."

She stared at him with those sympathetic brown eyes for so long he feared he would blurt out more deep shit, so he stood and poured himself some more scotch. Finally, she spoke. "This doesn't leave this room."

He returned to the table, eager to hear her side of the sex-scandal story. "No, ma'am."

"My ex wanted things he couldn't get from me, so he hired prostitutes to do them."

He hissed. "Bastard."

She seemed to warm to her topic, leaning toward him to confide even more. "He called them all Emily and made them wear brown-haired wigs and dress in nurse's outfits so they looked like me."

"That's sick. Was he kinky or something?"

"He wanted a threesome." She pounded a fist on the table. "Like one me wasn't enough."

"It's more than enough."

She pointed at him so close her finger grazed his cheek. "Thank you!" She licked another Frito, her pink little tongue driving him crazy. She met his eyes over the Frito. "He wanted to spank me and…"

He was almost afraid to speak. "And?"

"And screw me in the ass when I have a perfectly serviceable vagina for just that purpose!"

He forced a straight face. "I'm sure it's perfectly serviceable."

"Damn straight!" She beamed at him. "You're so easy to talk to. He screwed my neighbor and former best friend at the same time a week before the wedding." She jabbed a thumb at herself. "I'm the idiot that went through with it. I believed him that it was a drunken fluke and would never happen again."

He took her hand. "You're not an idiot. You just didn't want to lose the deposit on the wedding reception."

She laughed, which made him smile. She shouldn't have had to go through all that.

He went on. "The caterer, the DJ. That ball was rolling."

She gave him a watery smile that made his chest ache.

"C'mere," he said gently.

She didn't move.

He squeezed her hand. "I'm not kinky. I'm a real old-fashioned guy that likes good old missionary position. A few other positions too since we're being so honest. I'm perfectly content with a serviceable vagina."

"I'm not sleeping with you." She leaned a little closer, gave him a soft kiss, and smiled.

"Of course not." *More, please.*

As if she'd heard his silent entreaty, she slid onto his lap and snuggled her head into his chest. With all the scotch she'd downed, sex was a no-go, but he did like holding her. Maybe a little more kissing too. "So it's been two years," he said, "and did anyone appeal in any way?"

She laughed and looked up at him. "I sense you're fishing for compliments."

"No-o-oo. Unless you have one."

She shook her head, smiling.

He tapped the end of her nose. "Have you been with anyone since your ex?"

She let out a big sigh. "At first, no. But after a year, well, I have needs." She peered into his eyes super close. "You know?"

He nodded and tightened his hold on her. "I know."

She sighed. "He was…everything I hoped for. The exact opposite of my ex."

"What happened?"

"Same old story. Girl loves guy—" her voice came out small, and he leaned closer so he wouldn't miss a word "—guy loves someone else." She lifted her head, bumping his chin. "I sure can pick 'em, huh?"

He rubbed his chin. Wow. She had terrible luck. "How long were you with this guy? The one you, uh, loved?"

"Four months," she mumbled.

"Was it one of the doctors? Is that why you don't date doctors?" *Why did you turn me down?*

She regarded him quizzically. "I don't have anything against doctors. He was a school social worker."

The hairs on the back of his neck stood up. That wasn't a common job for a man. His stepbrother, Angel, was a school social worker. But as far as he knew, Angel hadn't dated anyone in years. They all thought he was in love with his best friend Julia. *Oh shit. Guy loves someone else.*

He cleared his throat. "What was his name?"

"Angel," she said on a sigh.

He quickly slid her off his lap and back to her own chair. He stood, speechless for a moment as he tried to slam the brakes on where he thought this thing between them was heading. Finally, just to be sure, he asked, "Angel Marino?"

"Yes." She went back to licking a Frito.

He started pacing the kitchen, let out a stream of curses, and shoved a hand in his hair. Why did the first woman he actually felt something for in a year have to be involved with his brother? She *loved* Angel. Dammit. He'd never admitted anything vulnerable like that commitment crap to anyone before. He slumped back into his chair.

"What's wrong?" she asked before popping the Frito in her mouth.

"That's my damned brother!"

"Stepbrother."

His head reared back. "You knew we were related?"

She waved a hand in the air. "Well, you know, Marino. He said Vince was his brother when I asked him about having the same name, and since you're Vince's stepbrother, I put it together."

"And that doesn't bother you?"

Her nose wrinkled adorably. "Why should it?"

"We grew up together since we were eight years old! Same age, shared a room, went to school together. How did you meet him? Did Vince introduce you?"

"No. One of his students became a patient. He stopped by to visit him, we got to talking, one thing led to another…"

He held up a hand. "Don't tell me anything else. Fuck me. I can't sleep with you now!"

She chomped a Frito. "Who asked you to?"

Angel was like a damned priest minus the celibacy apparently! His stepbrother was sensitive, patient, and comfortable talking about emotions and deep stuff most guys would never bring up. Women loved him for it. Angel was a woman's ideal kind of guy. Jared was a *guy* guy. He was rough around the edges, never knew when to stop with the joking, crossing the line into inappropriate territory with no clue that he had. He was hopeless in talking about feelings and shit.

He slapped a hand on the table. "If Angel was perfect for you, I'm sure as hell not."

"No kidding," she muttered.

"Then what'd you kiss me for?" he demanded.

"I don't know. For helping me?"

He huffed and stood. "This is over."

She looked up at him, a puzzled expression on her beautiful face. "What's over?"

"This." He gestured between them. "Whatever we had between us is over."

She yawned. "Okay." She stood, and he thought she was going to leave. Instead she walked into the living room, stretched out on the sofa and fell sound asleep.

*Damn, damn, damn.* He got a blanket and covered her with it. She sighed and curled into it.

He tore his gaze away from her sweet flushed cheeks, her glossy brown hair. He couldn't have her, and that was final. He could never do that to his brother.

He went outside and sat on his half-finished deck, thinking his bad luck might've just topped hers in the love department. Not that he loved her. Well, he didn't have the chance to. He dropped his head in his hands and groaned.

**5**

———————

Emily had a really good week. The press had moved on after she issued a statement saying no reconciliation was ever going to happen. Her ex pronounced it a misunderstanding and used the spotlight to talk more about himself. She doubted voters would get behind him again. So that was all good and, in standing up for herself, she felt some of her old confidence returning. Enough to make her think she could handle getting back on the horse with the only man to give her a little giddyup in a very long time—Jared.

There was a sizzling attraction between them, no question. He'd admitted his rep was true—he was a good-time guy with serious commitment issues. And she was looking for a good time. She wouldn't hurt him with a onetime deal, and there was no way she'd get her heart broken. Besides, after seeing him at his cozy house surrounded by the furniture he made with his own hands, she trusted him. He was steady and stable and honest about what he did and why. It made everything so simple—fun and flirty and light—exactly what she needed.

And he'd been so good to her too. After she slept for three hours on his living room sofa last Saturday, he'd let her relax at his house while he walked back to the hospital and got her work shirt and her car. She drove the short distance home, feeling refreshed, and returned the call of the biggest-name news station to issue her statement over the phone.

She eagerly looked forward to the Saturday morning Captain Cuddle visit with Jared. Maybe she'd sneak out the service exit and walk home with him again. Wasn't that what all his nurse flings did? It would all be normal procedure for him.

As soon as she saw Jared enter the ward in his Captain Cuddle costume, she crossed over to him with a big smile and handed him the goody bag. "Hey, Captain Cuddle, thanks again for your help last Saturday."

"Captain *Huddle.* No problem." He turned to go.

"Wait." She grabbed his arm and met hard muscle. Ooh, this was going to be so fun! "I get off at one." She lowered her voice to a sexy purr. "Maybe we could have lunch and hang out at your place again."

He slid out of reach and then spoke in a gravely serious tone made less serious by his porcupine hat with gray knitted quills sticking up all over. "Emily, we can only be friends."

"Sure," she said brightly. *Friends with benefits just once.* "So I'll meet you by the service elevator. Okay?"

He pushed his eye mask up and regarded her with his gorgeous green eyes. "Angel is my brother. I won't hurt him."

"It won't hurt him at all," she assured him. "It was a year ago. He dumped me. Besides I know your rep—" she winked "—and I'm okay with it." In fact, Angel hadn't even crossed her mind in so long she had to wonder if she really loved him or just appreciated him for being so different from her ex. She'd still been a bit of a mess back then.

He stepped close, leaning down to her ear, and her libido sped to a heated gallop. Boy, now that she'd opened the gates, it was lust city. "I'm sorry," he said quietly. "You don't know how sorry. But no." With that, he whirled away, cape flying out behind him as he strode into Chris's room. He always remembered that Chris was the sickest and needed the first visit before he fell asleep.

She stared after him for a moment, wondering if there was more to Dr. One-and-Done than she'd realized. Then she heard him bark, "Are you crazy? The Yankees suck. Boo-oo-oo." And quickly concluded he really was just the happy-go-lucky guy he seemed to be.

She'd have to ramp up her efforts where Jared was concerned. Angel was a nonissue from her point of view. He'd been the one to let her go a year ago, and it wasn't like Angel would ever find out she slept with Jared one time. Hell, she deserved to have some fun in her life. Didn't she?

Only when she got off her shift, Jared was nowhere to be found.

As soon as Jared got off Captain Huddle duty at noon, he called Angel. Luckily his stepbrother was on his way home from tutoring, and they agreed to meet at Angel's place. He tossed the costume bag and books on the floor of his truck and drove to Angel's apartment. He lived in what used to be an art studio on the back property of a large contemporary-style home in Fieldridge. Angel had taken the apartment because his best friend, Julia, and her husband, Brad, had bought a house in Fieldridge when they'd first married. Angel had always needed to be close to Julia, and Julia had always delighted in having him close. She still lived in that house across town.

He parked in the street out front and went around back to ring the bell. No answer. He looked around and didn't see his brother's ancient black Honda Civic. Jared had driven pedal to the metal to get here fast. He sat down on the concrete step of the studio apartment to wait. He had to find out what Angel thought of the Emily situation. She'd made him an offer today, actually seeming eager to hook up. As if she'd thought over his one-and-done rep and thought it might be fun. He wasn't at all sure one time would be enough. After she'd left his place last weekend, his house felt kind of… empty. But if one time wasn't enough, when would it end? He just kept thinking of her being in love with Angel. And poor Angel being in love with Julia but never having her. The more he thought about it, the more he thought Emily needed someone like Angel after her awful cheating bastard of a husband. There weren't too many great guys like Angel in the world. And maybe Angel needed her too. They deserved each other.

So why did he feel sick to his stomach at the thought?

He stood when he saw Angel pull into the driveway. His stepbrother got out of the car in a black leather jacket open over a white cotton T-shirt and jeans, holding a briefcase full of papers. Wholesome, that was what he was. His dark brown hair was always rumpled and his dark brown eyes were always kind. Yes, this was definitely the sort of man Emily deserved.

Angel caught sight of Jared and smiled his angelic, dimpled smile. "Hey, Jare, did you eat?"

"Nope."

Angel crossed the stretch of yard to the studio apartment. His stepbrother was only an inch shorter than his own five foot eleven, but lean and lithe, which always made him seem smaller. Jared had looked out for him at school, making sure no one messed with him, and still felt a little protective of Angel's tender heart.

"Why so serious?" Angel asked when he reached him. He put the key in the door and opened it, gesturing for Jared to go in ahead of him.

"No reason."

"How's grilled cheese sound?"

"Good."

"All right. Just give me a minute." He set his briefcase on one of the wicker dining room chairs surrounding the rectangular wood table. The studio space was large and open with lots of windows and two skylights. The hardwood floors still had some splatters of paint on them. Angel used half the space as a dining room and the other half as a living room with a large futon sofa that pulled out into a bed. A TV sat on a small stand in the corner. The coffee table was an old trunk. It had a Bohemian college feel to it. Jared knew it was because

Angel saved all of his meager social worker salary toward buying a house one day.

"I'll help," Jared said.

Angel smiled and winked. "I got it. Sit down and relax. You look stressed. Everything okay at work?" He headed for his small kitchen. A half wall separated the kitchen from the rest of the space.

That was Angel for you. Always thinking of others. Always asking how they were. Emily definitely deserved Angel. He just had to give Angel a little shove in that direction.

He helped himself to a beer in Angel's fridge, which was stocked full of healthy food. He grabbed a handful of already washed grapes too. "Work's fine," he said, popping a grape in his mouth before tossing a grape into Angel's open mouth.

"Yeah?" Angel pulled out a frying pan. "So what's up?"

"Nothing."

Angel brushed by him, giving him a disbelieving look before pulling out sliced cheese and butter from the fridge. "I hardly ever see you on a Saturday afternoon. You're usually too busy in the service of Venus."

Jared snorted. That was their little joke. It was a historic euphemism for sex. He and his fraternity brothers used to toss around a bunch of hysterical old-timey euphemisms for sex back in college. Venus was the goddess of love, and though Jared didn't love the women he hooked up with, he treated them like goddesses in the bedroom. Thus, the lack of complaints thrown in his direction when he bailed. Usually he met up with a nurse at the service exit after their shift and walked them to his house. Exactly as Emily wanted to do today.

Not gonna happen.

He took a long pull on his beer and watched Angel as he prepared the sandwiches.

"So it looks like we'll have a full house for Thanksgiving," Angel said over his shoulder. "Everyone's going to be there and Kennedy's whole family too." Kennedy was his older brother Luke's fiancée, a petite blond female version of Luke

—ambitious, sharp, a real go-getter in wealth management, yet devoted to family and helping others. His brother was ridiculously happy.

Jared grunted. "We'll have to be at Gabe's place to fit everyone." That was the house he and his brothers had grown up in, a large Victorian in Clover Park.

The frying pan sizzled and Angel dropped a couple of sandwiches onto it. He spoke over his shoulder. "Pretty soon we'll need a kids table too." So far there was only his oldest brother Gabe's (and Zoe's) ten-month-old son, Miles, but now Sophia was pregnant. Nico and Lily would be popping one out soon.

"Julia coming too?" Jared asked casually. Even though everyone knew Angel was in love with her, he wouldn't touch her on account of their twisted relationship. She'd been married to his friend Brad, who'd died overseas during his tour of duty. Angel had promised to look after Julia if Brad didn't make it back. He'd been doing just that for the last five years.

Angel stiffened almost imperceptibly before grabbing a spatula. "No. She'll be at her parents' house. They live over in New Medford, about a forty-minute drive."

Jared drank some more beer, needing the liquid courage, before blurting, "What about Emily?"

"Who?" Angel kept cooking, his back to Jared, which irritated him. He needed to read his expression. Angel was incapable of lying and had the worst poker face in history.

Jared crossed to Angel's side. "Emily Maguire."

Angel raised a brow. "How do you know Emily?"

"You mean how do I know you *slept* with her?"

"No," Angel responded calmly. "I mean how do you know her?"

"I met her at work. She's a nurse, *as you know*." He raised his brows, waiting for Angel to explain himself.

"Oh. Tell her I said hi."

He slammed his beer bottle on the counter. "Hi? She's in love with you and that's all you have to say for yourself."

"I haven't seen Emily in a year!" Angel threw the spatula

down, left the frying sandwiches, and got himself a beer. He grabbed the bottle opener, popped the top, and drank.

They stared each other down for a long tension-filled moment.

Angel broke the silence. "It's none of your damned business anyway."

Smoke started fuming off the frying pan. Angel rushed over and flipped the sandwiches, which were blackened, the cheese melting over the sides. He finished cooking them, slid the sandwiches onto plates, and inclined his head at Jared. "Take my beer to the table."

Jared brought over the beer, and Angel joined him a minute later with the sandwiches. They started eating in silence.

"I can't believe you've been secretly dating all this time," Jared finally said half accusingly.

Angel slapped a hand on the table. "I'm not a fucking priest or a monk or any of those idiotic labels everyone sticks on me." He took a pull on his beer. "And I'm not angelic despite my nickname, which, by the way, my mom gave me as a baby and it stuck. My name is Angelo, and I'm no saint."

You could've knocked Jared over with a rosary. He thought he'd known Angel so well. Yet all these years he had this whole other side of him that none of them had ever seen. Maybe because no one had ever thought to look.

"But you have such a sweet face," Jared said, pinching Angel's clean-shaven cheek. "Look at these dimples."

Angel slapped his hand away. "Look in the mirror. You've got the dimpled smile too."

True. And they didn't even have the same parents.

"So you just what…" Jared studied Angel like he'd never really seen him before. *Was he just as much a horndog as the rest of them?* "You just go around secretly dating?"

Angel leaned back in his seat. "I try to date. You know? Julia—" he laid a hand over his heart "—she's got me good. But she's still grieving. Once in a while I try to move on, go on a date or two—"

"Or four months."

He inclined his head. "Or four months, though that's rare. But then no matter how nice the woman is, I just realize I can't ever love them because—"

"Julia."

Angel nodded once and took a long swallow of beer.

"But why do you keep it secret?" Jared asked.

"Because," he croaked and then cleared his throat, "deep down I know there's no future. I don't want to lead them on with Sunday dinner, holidays, all that."

"So you've never slept with Julia all this time?" Jared asked. That was saintly love in his book.

"Welp." Angel's lips formed a flat line. "We've had our moments, but, in the end, that's just not enough."

"Never?" Jared pressed because he didn't know what the hell a "moment" meant.

Angel swallowed visibly. "In a weak moment. A couple of weak moments." Now Jared understood. Angel scrubbed a hand over his face. "We both regretted it."

This was terrible. Angel couldn't let Julia go, yet he couldn't move forward with her. Emily's words ran on repeat in his head, *girl loves guy, guy loves someone else*. Except the *someone else*, Julia, was never going to happen. Hadn't Angel suffered long enough with that one-sided kind of love? He pinched the bridge of his nose as the words *girl loves guy* screamed through his head. He wished he didn't know all this, wished he'd met Emily in another universe that didn't involve his stepbrother.

"You okay?" Angel asked.

"Yeah." Jared went back to his lunch, trying to think of the right words to convince Angel that he should be with Emily. None came to him.

He watched his stepbrother eat, seeming resigned to his lot in life.

"Emily's great," Jared finally said once he finished his sandwich.

Angel nodded. "I know. I really liked her. Sometimes I think I messed up...like, maybe I shouldn't have bailed, but…" He rubbed the back of his neck. "Ah, it's too late, anyway. I don't want to screw up with Emily again."

Dammit. See? Angel regretted bailing. Jared knew the right thing to do, felt it deep in his churning gut. He had to convince Angel to give Emily a second chance. Then he'd have to convince Emily that Angel was worth the risk. He immediately shot that talking-to-Emily idea down. Nope. He couldn't be alone with her long enough for a heart-wrenching talk without lust messing with his head. Let Angel convince her to take that risk. Jared would just make sure Angel didn't screw up.

"She's just like you in a lot of ways," Jared said quietly. "Kind, smart, great with kids." He looked out the large kitchen window over the sink, remembering how beautiful she'd looked sleeping on his sofa. Her glossy brown hair spread out around her. Her sweet lips parted slightly in sleep.

"Jare?"

He snapped his attention back to Angel. "She's the total package. And she loves you. She told me so. Give her a second chance, and don't screw it up this time."

Angel held up a hand. "I'm not sure—"

"She needs someone like you. Her ex, well, you've seen the news. A sick cheating bastard. I mean what kind of guy orders up hookers to cheat on his wife and then makes them all pretend to be his wife so he can spank them and—"

"What?"

Jared clamped his mouth shut. That might've been one of those this-doesn't-leave-this-room confessions brought on by too much scotch. "Forget I said that. My point is—" he pointed at Angel "—you should give it another shot. Ask her to dinner."

Angel's brows drew together. "Why don't you ask her to dinner?"

"She doesn't want someone like me. She needs someone like you."

Angel wiped his mouth with a napkin. "What's wrong with you?"

"Nothing. I'm just not…" He crossed his arms, steeling

himself against whatever Angel might say to push him in Emily's direction. It would be too easy to cave with the amount of lust he'd been fighting ever since he met her. "I'm too much of the good-time guy."

"And what am I? The good-for-you guy?"

Jared jabbed a hand in the air. "Yes!"

Angel studied him for a long moment. "You're a good guy too. Don't let anyone tell you differently."

A rare heat crept up his neck. "Nah."

"We were raised the same way," Angel said. "With kindness. That's what we both put out in the world. Look at what you do for a living. You make people whole again, give them a chance to use their hands or walk again without pain. Not everyone can do what you do. I'd probably puke the minute I had to slice into someone, but you…you get right in there and you do a good job. I'm just good at talking. You're good at doing."

Jared waved that away. "But you're so good at the sensitive-guy thing. And…I don't think I could hook up with her after she hooked up with you. Bros before hos, right?" He lifted his beer bottle to clink against Angel's.

Angel shook his head and didn't clink bottles. "Don't say hos. Come on."

Jared grinned. "But chicks doesn't rhyme with bros."

Angel tossed the crust of his sandwich at him. "Hate to break it to you, but, unless you got yourself a virgin, every woman you date's already slept with someone. Besides, I wore a condom and closed my eyes the whole time." He covered his eyes with one hand. "Emily who?"

"Hardi-har-har. Ask her to dinner."

Angel dropped his hand. "Why do you care so damn much?"

"I want you to be happy. I'm just asking you to give her another chance. She's…" He found himself smiling, thinking of Emily. "She's special."

One corner of Angel's mouth lifted. He stood and gathered the plates. "Okay, you convinced me. I'll ask her to dinner."

Jared clenched his jaw and then forced himself to relax. Sometimes it hurt to do the right thing. That was all. "Great." And that was as far as he could get without throttling his stepbrother for doing exactly what he'd asked him to. "I'm going to go."

"Already?"

He was halfway out the door when he said over his shoulder, "Good luck."

Angel barked out a laugh. "I won't need luck!"

Jared cringed and bolted.

**6**

---

Jared was a little late to Sunday family dinner because he'd been working on his deck all weekend. The more he thought about Angel taking Emily out to dinner and probably hooking up with her, the more he wanted to pound nails. He'd finished nearly the whole deck. All he had left to do was the railing and steps leading down to the yard. He was physically exhausted, and his brain was tired of running the same hamster-wheel scenario where he ended up best man at Angel and Emily's wedding for being the damned genius who brought them together.

He didn't bother to ring the bell, just headed on in to Gabe's house, where he'd grown up and knew like the back of his hand. Their dog, Fred, sped to the foyer in a blur of fluffy silver and black fur, barking ferociously. Jared stroked the dog behind the ear, and Fred immediately settled down.

"Come on," he said, and the dog trotted after him. The furniture and decorating in the house was different than when he'd lived there. Gabe had put in his own modern-style furniture and his wife, Zoe, had decorated with lots of jazz concert posters. She was a jazz singer, probably one of the world's best.

"I'm here!" he announced when he hit the dining room. Fred scooted back to his place under the table, hoping someone would drop some food. "Let the party…" He trailed off in shock at seeing Emily sitting next to Angel at Sunday family dinner. Angel said he never invited women home because he knew deep down they had no future. Yet there she was, smiling at him.

"Hi, Jared," she said, her brown eyes bright. She wore a lacy pink sweater that gave him a clear view of her cleavage peeking out of a matching silky shirt with skinny straps.

"Emily!" He forced his gaze up to her eyes. What did this mean? Could she and Angel be serious after just one dinner? Well, they had dated for four whole months. He just stood there, frozen in place, staring as shock slowly gave way to despair.

"Son, have a seat," his stepdad, Vinny, said.

He slipped into the only empty chair next to Gabe and stared at his plate. Conversation resumed, but he couldn't speak or eat or anything. Someone passed him the baked ziti, and he scooped some on his plate automatically. Emily's laugh rang out and he lifted his head to see Angel and Emily across the table, smiling at each other. And then a white-hot rage surged through him. What the hell! Angel didn't have to flaunt her in front of him. He should've gone back to quietly dating her so none of them had to witness the lovey-dovey crap. At least until they were married, making her off-limits permanently.

"You couldn't have taken her out to dinner anywhere but here?" he hissed across the table at Angel.

Angel cocked his head, the picture of angelic innocence. Ha! Jared was onto him now. "Maybe we should speak privately," Angel said in an infuriatingly calm voice.

"Fine." Jared threw down his napkin and headed for the living room, which was more private than the kitchen open to the dining room.

He heard his mom ask, "What was that about?"

And his stepdad's grumbled reply, "Who knows? They'll work it out."

Angel appeared a moment later, all smiles. He'd even

dressed up for his special date in a light blue button-down shirt and dress pants. "Hey, Jare."

Jared wanted to punch that smile off his face. "Hey, *Angelo*." He sure as hell was no angel. "I see you're in full horndog mode."

Angel bit back a smile. His dimples totally gave him away. "I have no idea what you're talking about."

He jabbed him in the chest and wished he could glower down at him, but they were nearly the same size. "You're flaunting your relationship with her. It's not enough I hand her over on a silver platter, you have to show up here to rub my nose in it."

Angel held up his palms. "You're the one who told me to ask her to dinner. I asked her to dinner."

"Why here?"

Angel lifted one shoulder up and down. "It was free."

"Free! She deserves a nice restaurant. What? You couldn't afford it?" He pulled out his wallet and grabbed some bills. "Take it and get out of here." Never mind the fact that Jared had suggested dinner. Seeing it happen in front of his eyes made him feel like a raging bull. Angel was supposed to quietly do the right thing by Emily far away from him.

Angel shook his head. "I'm not taking your money. Can we eat?"

Jared shoved a hand in his hair, working hard to speak in a reasonable voice. "Are you serious about her? Is that why she's here?"

"Nah. Not serious."

He grabbed him by the shirt and got in his face, all reason flying out the window. "She deserves better than someone whose heart is already taken. Don't play with her." He fiercely regretted pushing Angel toward Emily. Angel was screwing it up already. He wasn't even serious about her! That thought should've been welcome, but all he could think about was Emily getting hurt again. Jared never should've gotten involved in all this touchy-feely stuff.

Angel's kind brown eyes met his. "I hear ya loud and clear, brother."

Jared let go of Angel's shirt. What was he doing? This was his brother. Bros before chicks. He couldn't believe he was threatening his saint of a brother.

"Sorry," he mumbled and returned to the dining room, prepared to suffer through a long meal.

Emily exchanged a small smile with Angel, who was grinning devilishly from behind Jared's back as they returned to the dining room. Angel had called her yesterday and rather dutifully told her that Jared thought Angel should ask her to dinner. So dutifully that she didn't believe for a minute he actually wanted to.

"I want Jared," she'd said in a bold move, surprising herself. Guess she was serious about a fun fling. The nice thing about Angel's social worker background was, you could tell him anything, and he'd take it in stride. The man heard some doozies from his clients.

"So, you want his number or…"

"No. I'll see him at work. He has a good thing going with the service exit revolving door of flings and I'm ready to sign up."

"Emily."

"What?"

"That doesn't sound like you."

She blew out a breath. "I'm tired of being the stoic good girl. I want to have fun again. Just once. Jared's good at that."

"He is the good-time guy."

"Exactly."

"Why don't you come to our Sunday family dinner tomorrow night? Jared'll be there. You could probably go home with him. Let the good times roll."

"That is an excellent idea." She paused. "You don't think it's going to be weird or awkward or something because I was with you before? You know, for all of us to be at the same table?"

"That'll be the best part."

"You devil."

He chuckled. Angel's devilish streak was one of the things that had appealed to her about him. He was a good guy, so that made it a safe way to be near a little bit of naughtiness.

Angel went on. "Seriously, though, he needs to see with his own eyes that you and I are no longer an item. Then he'll be willing to…well, whatever you want, I guess."

But tonight wasn't going the way she'd hoped. She thought she and Jared might have a little verbal sparring, some lively conversation, but instead Jared was sullen. Angel, by her side, was positively gleeful.

She was never going to get her fling.

"It's so nice to meet a friend of Angel's, finally," Zoe said, giving Emily a sunny smile. She was married to Jared's older brother Gabe. She'd discovered earlier from Angel that Gabe, Luke, and Jared were biological brothers with the same light brown to blond hair and dark blue eyes. Except Jared, who had those amazing green eyes. Their mom had married their Italian stepdad, Vinny. Jared's stepbrothers—Vince, Nico, and Angel—had dark brown hair and dark brown eyes. All of them gorgeous, but Nico, she had to admit upon meeting him, was breathtaking with movie-star good looks. He only had eyes for his redheaded wife, Lily.

Zoe went on, her brown eyes sparkling with excitement. "We were starting to get worried about Angel, but here you are!"

"Here I am," Emily said weakly with a sideways glance at Angel and a silent urgent message *help me out here.*

Angel smiled and kept eating his baked ziti.

"So how long have you been together?" Zoe asked.

Emily looked around the table as the entire family—Mrs. Marino, Mr. Marino, Gabe, Zoe, Vince, Sophia, Luke and his fiancée, Kennedy, Nico, Lily, and Jared stared at her expectantly. Even baby Miles had quieted in his high chair to stare at her with a fist full of noodle in his mouth. Angel was still eating, unperturbed.

She looked right at Jared. "We're not together."

Jared glared at Angel and mumbled something under his breath she couldn't quite catch.

"Oh," Zoe said, shooting a quick look to her husband, Gabe. "So it's like that."

Now they all thought she was just sleeping with Angel. She turned to Angel for help.

"Anyone want more bread?" Angel asked. Before anyone could answer, he left the room, saying over his shoulder, "I'll get it."

She picked up her fork. "This is excellent ziti." She dug in, shoving a big forkful in her mouth.

There was an awkward silence.

"Angel," Vince said, shaking his head, "who knew?"

His brothers laughed. Vince's wife, Sophia, elbowed him and hissed, "I told you."

"How're you feeling, Sophia?" Mrs. Marino asked.

"As long as I stick to bread, I'm good," Sophia said, holding up her slice of unbuttered plain Italian bread.

"I'm trying to steer her toward starches and small portions of protein," Vince said. "Plenty of fluids, of course. We're still finding out her triggers. We know to avoid strong odors, and fish seems to be—"

"Do you hear yourself?" Nico asked on a laugh.

"Do you want to meet your dinner up close?" Vince threatened.

Nico laughed harder until his wife, Lily, put a hand on his arm. He turned and kissed her temple. She smiled.

"So how long have you, um, known Angel?" Sophia asked Emily diplomatically.

"They dated for four months a year ago," Jared announced.

Sophia's jaw dropped. "Really?"

Emily looked for Angel, who appeared very busy in the kitchen and still wasn't coming to her rescue. "We, uh, broke up."

"Why?" Zoe asked. "I mean, maybe since he invited you to Sunday dinner, he—"

"Just friends," Angel announced, returning with the bread.

Jared glared at Angel and mimicked, "Just friends," in a singsong voice.

Oh-kay. Emily was a little confused. Wasn't it good if she and Angel were just friends so she and Jared could hook up?

Luke looked between Jared and Angel. "This is messed up."

Kennedy, a lovely petite blond woman, piped up at Luke's side. "So, Emily, tell us about your work at the hospital. You're some kind of nurse, you said?"

Emily smiled at Kennedy, relieved to have someone willing to smooth things over, and told her all about the programs she was working on to help make the children's stay easier.

Finally, the whole awkward evening ended. Angel had enjoyed himself a little too much. She shot him a dark look that only made him smile more. Jared was making a beeline for the door, and she hurried to catch up with him.

"Wait up," she said.

He kept going.

"Jared! Could you give me a ride home?"

He stopped short and slowly turned. "Why can't Angel do it?" He jabbed a finger behind her. She glanced over her shoulder to find Angel standing there already wearing his leather jacket. He winked at her, and she quickly turned back to Jared. "Didn't you come with him?" Jared barked.

She crossed to Jared's side. "Yes, but I thought maybe I could ride home with you. He won't mind."

"I don't mind," Angel said, appearing at her side. He smiled his devilish, dimpled smile.

Jared smacked him upside the head.

"Jared!" she exclaimed.

Angel smacked Jared upside the head.

"Angel!" she exclaimed.

Jared pushed up his sleeves and advanced on Angel. She backed away as the two men circled each other in the foyer.

"Um, help?" she called to whatever family member might

want to intervene. "Mrs. Marino! I think someone's going to get hurt!"

The family rushed in to see Angel peeling off his leather jacket and tossing it to the floor in a big show of machismo. Their fluffy dog, Fred, growled, ran over, and started humping the jacket.

"Please don't fight," Emily said. "This has all been just a big misunderstanding."

"Whoa," Nico said.

"Twenty on Jared," Luke said.

"I got fifty on Angel," Vince declared proudly. "I taught him every dirty trick I know."

The brothers quickly placed bets about evenly split between Jared and Angel.

"Boys!" Mrs. Marino exclaimed, hands on her hips. "What do you think you're doing betting on your own brothers?"

"Men!" Mr. Marino barked. "Take it outside."

Emily's eyes widened as Angel held the door open and gestured for Jared to go outside first. Jared grabbed Angel and shoved him out the door. All the men rushed through after them to watch. She wasn't sure if she could stand to see either one of them get hurt.

She turned to Mrs. Marino. "Shouldn't we stop them?"

"I get the feeling only you can stop them," Mrs. Marino said. "They're fighting over you."

"This is ridiculous," Emily muttered. This kind of thing would never happen with her and her older sisters. They would just silently seethe and convey everything with a lethal look. Men were beasts.

She stomped outside to find Jared had Angel in a headlock on the front lawn. "Jared! Let him go."

"You'd like that," Jared snapped and then grunted as Angel got in a jab to the kidneys that made Jared release his hold.

"I taught him that," Vince said proudly and put Gabe in a headlock, who elbowed him in the kidneys too. "Oof," Vince said and then grinned.

Emily rushed in between Jared and Angel, who were

circling each other again. "Angel, tell him there's nothing between us."

"I did," Angel said. "He's too thickheaded to listen."

"Jared," she said gently, "please don't fight. Could you just take me home? I'd really like a ride home with you."

"Your girlfriend needs a ride home," Jared barked before turning and stalking off to his truck.

And before she could say *I'm not his girlfriend*, he'd taken off in a big squeal of tires.

"That was disappointing," Luke said. "Who won?"

The brothers began arguing over what should count for points. Angel just shook his head and turned to her. "C'mon, I'll take you home."

On the drive home with Angel, she felt horribly guilty. "I shouldn't have come tonight. I feel terrible that you and Jared got into a fight."

"Don't feel bad," he said. "Sometimes things get physical. Testosterone and all that."

He was awfully casual about the whole thing. "What if one of you got hurt?"

"Come on, it's Jared. You think he's going to bust up his hand on my ugly mug? He would never risk it because then he couldn't do surgery."

"So you knew all along he wouldn't hurt you?"

"Just blowing off steam."

She folded her hands in her lap and stared straight ahead. Men were a strange lot. She'd really been worried. "He seems so mad, though. How am I going to have fun with him when he's like that?"

Angel glanced over at her and grinned. "It's good for him. Gives him a little challenge. Normally women just fall into his lap."

"That's what I was trying to do!"

"Wouldn't recommend it."

"Well, your way sucked."

He chuckled. "Fine, do it your way."

"I will."

"He works office hours ten to six on the third floor of the

hospital Monday, Tuesday, Thursday. Maybe you could catch him then. Wednesday is surgery day and too busy. He usually eats lunch in the cafeteria at one."

She let out a breath of relief. Angel was finally helping her. "Okay, thank you."

Angel smiled his dimpled smile at her. "Sure. And mention you're thinking of doing a freebase jump. He's a total adrenaline junkie. He'll probably want to do it with you."

"What's that?"

"It's when you rock climb with a parachute and then jump."

"Sounds dangerous, but, hmm…maybe I'll mention it."

"Definitely mention it. He loves that stuff. But only do it if Jared's with you, okay? Let him take the lead. He's the expert."

"Okay. Thanks, Angel."

He smiled widely. "No problem at all."

Emily headed to the hospital cafeteria for lunch at one o'clock the very next day, hoping to see Jared. She stood in line for food and kept checking around. Finally he arrived, standing several people behind her in line with another doctor. She waved.

He raised his hand in acknowledgement and went back to his conversation.

She got her food, paid, and waited by the cashier for Jared to catch up. When he stopped to pay, she asked, "Mind if I sit with you?"

He stiffened. "Actually I'm getting this to go."

She looked at his tray with a burger and fruit salad on a ceramic plate with no take-out containers. "You are?"

"Yeah, crazy day." He shoved a twenty-dollar bill at the cashier. "Keep the change." And then he took off, tray in hand.

He'd just given the cashier a twelve-dollar tip in the self-serve cafeteria. Was he avoiding her because she showed up with Angel for dinner last night, or was he really busy today?

"Jared, wait!"

He kept going, picking up the pace. "Tell Angel I said hi."

"I'm not seeing Angel," she called to his retreating back.

Okay. She'd try again tomorrow.

Tuesday wasn't much better. She got to the cafeteria a little after one, and Jared was already sitting at a table full of doctors. She walked right by his table with a cheery hello and, though he smiled and said hello, he immediately returned to his table conversation. Like he didn't really want to talk to her. Had she imagined the chemistry between them? No, she'd definitely felt something really strong. That couldn't have just been her. Maybe she needed to explain better about Angel.

She took a seat across the cafeteria with her supervisor, Jane, and surreptitiously checked Jared out, but he was very focused on his turkey sandwich and didn't look up once. At least she still had that ace in the hole Angel had told her about—freebase jumping. Jared was the good-time guy and an adrenaline junkie. She had his number. No way Dr. One-and-Done could resist freebase jumping followed by a little nurse action. She just had to make him understand Angel wasn't standing between them in any way.

Jared entered the hospital cafeteria on Thursday at his usual time and quickly looked around for Emily. No sign of her. He relaxed a little. On Monday she'd wanted to sit with him, and on Tuesday she'd watched him from across the room. Thankfully, he spent Wednesday in surgery. He was used to women finding him when they wanted a little fun, but Emily was in a whole different league. The friend league. Besides, he could only stay strong in his resolve to resist her if he kept a safe distance.

He'd nearly made it to the pork lo mein when someone tapped his shoulder. He turned and there she was, looking all kinds of sexy with her glossy brown hair, sparkling brown eyes, and blue scrubs with elephants holding trunks. Her sexy body hiding under scrubs tempted him way too much.

"Hi," she said with an impish smile.

"Hi."

"So, I hope you're not mad at me for sitting next to Angel at dinner. We're just friends."

"Uh-huh."

"No, really."

He turned back around, ignoring her. Angel wouldn't have invited her to dinner if he was thinking just friends. He hadn't brought Julia by for Sunday dinner with the family in years. Not since the early days when she'd first lost her husband and couldn't tolerate being alone.

"I'll sit with you today," Emily said. "And don't tell me you're too busy to sit with a friend."

He blew out a breath and said over his shoulder, "Fine." He could only avoid her for so long working at the same hospital. Although, now that he thought about it, he couldn't remember seeing her in the hospital cafeteria before. He definitely would've remembered a beautiful, sexy nurse like her. Why was it so hard to do the right thing?

He led the way to a table by the window, and she settled across from him.

She took a sip of water and looked up at him from under her lashes. He knew that look. It was a flirtatious gesture right before a suggestive statement. He shoved lo mein in his mouth and looked out the window.

"Maybe we could have lunch at your house on Saturday after your Captain Cuddle visit," she said.

"Captain *Huddle*," he said around a mouthful of noodles. If he had to dress up in a ridiculous costume, at least he could own it. He was a hedgehog, dammit.

"Captain Huddle, of course."

He could hear the smile in her voice and met her sparkling brown eyes. "So-o-o," she said with a small smile, "lunch at your place? I'll cook as a thank you for your help with my narrow escape from those reporters. I'm a pretty good cook."

She flipped her hair over her shoulder. Another classic flirtatious move. "Or you could come to my place?"

He had to shut this down though it went against every lusty instinct. There was no way in hell he could be alone with her and just be friends. In fact, that would be hell. "I'm busy."

"Oh." She went back to her lunch, looking surprisingly crushed.

"Thanks anyway," he added.

"I'm thinking of doing a freebase jump this weekend," she said brightly. "It sounds thrilling. Well, you know, you're the expert."

He cocked his head. "I'm the what?"

"You're the adrenaline junkie, right? You do stuff like that all the time. Maybe—"

He set his fork down. "That's dangerous. People die doing freebase jumps. You are not doing a freebase jump." He'd never risked it himself and he'd done a lot of crazy shit.

"I just wanted to have a little fun." She rocked her head side to side. "Little excitement. You want to come with me?"

"Do I want—" He stopped himself as he realized he'd gotten loud. "I'm not doing a freebase jump. You're not doing a freebase jump. End of story." He'd never in his life dug in his heels like this, but some part of him wanted to roll Emily in bubble wrap and then tuck her safely behind him so he could shield her from any and all dangers. Geez, this super-hero stuff was going to his head.

"Well, I have to do something for excitement." She raised a brow, looking at him expectantly.

He racked his brain for something safe she could do that was also exciting. Skydiving was out. Too much for a newbie. Bungee jumping—too risky. He absolutely needed her safe and tried not to think too hard on the why, given that Angel was in the picture. Angel should really be the one stepping up to the plate here.

She gave him another sweet smile. "Or just cooking lunch for you could be exciting with the right spices. Zing! You like Mexican?"

She was just too adorable. *Zing.* "Yes, I like Mexican."

"Great!"

He scrubbed a hand over his face. "Just lunch and then I have to go. I've got a lot going on."

"Of course you do. Lotta nurses lined up—" she finger quoted and gave him a big exaggerated wink "— for the service of Venus."

He jolted and then narrowed his eyes. "Did Angel tell you that?" He never told anyone he called his hookups the service of Venus. That was his little joke with his brother. He hadn't been tempted even once by another woman since he met her nearly three weeks ago. And it wasn't for lack of offers, either. The whole thing was so aggravating, what with the Angel situation. And the fact that Jared kept running into her, lusting for her—

"Maybe," she said, grinning mischievously.

He ground his teeth, not liking one bit Emily and Angel talking about his sex life. Especially because he wasn't getting any! Could this situation be any more fucked up? "What else did you talk to Angel about?"

"Not much." She picked up her glass of iced tea, put the straw in her mouth, gazed into his eyes, and sucked. *Tease.* He adjusted himself under the table.

He picked up his fork and jabbed it in the lo mein. "So, you're…" *Single and looking? What was with all these flirty gestures? Wasn't she still with Angel? It had only been four days since their Sunday dinner. Was she still in love with Angel?* "Never mind. None of my business." He quickly finished his lo mein so he wouldn't blurt out any of his wayward thoughts.

He glanced at her eating a salad with a small smile on her beautiful heart-shaped face. Even her face stood for love. She deserved that, and Angel had said he wasn't serious about her. Was Jared just supposed to step back and watch Angel take Emily for a ride that would ultimately hurt her? But if Jared stepped up, would he end up hurting her too? He sucked at relationships.

She leaned forward and lowered her voice to a sexy purr. "What were you going to say? You can ask me anything."

He swallowed hard, feeling like he was standing in the open hatch of an airplane about to take a free fall into a happy parachute ride or a splat into death. Terrifying and exciting and absolutely no going back. Was Angel still between them? It was one thing for Angel to say there was nothing there, but he needed to know if Emily had really moved on. After that tense Sunday dinner, Jared knew he'd done the wrong thing pushing Angel and Emily together. Well, wrong for Angel, since he wasn't serious, but maybe right for Emily. He was so confused. But one thing was clear, after running into Emily so much at work this week, it had hit home just how much he wanted her. He was a selfish bastard, but there it was—he wanted her all to himself even if Angel was better for her.

She looked at him expectantly. His lust and like—really intense like—were making him tongue-tied. He should just lay it on the table and ask, *Are you over Angel?* But the words wouldn't come. Because what if she said no?

*Okay, okay. Think positive. Assume she is over Angel.* He started shredding his napkin as he worked up a good speech for that scenario. *I like you, and if I'm reading your signals right, you want to hook up, but this would* not *be just a hookup for me.*

"We'll go out for Mexican on Saturday," he blurted. "Bring Angel."

He watched her expression for any telltale signs of how she really felt about Angel. Why was he torturing himself like this? He shouldn't have given her the option. Damn guilt.

Her brown eyes twinkled with merriment. "Should I meet you at the service elevator after my shift on Saturday? Or the supply closet? That was fun."

He swept up the shredded napkin and stood, mad at himself for bringing Angel into it again, and mad at her for not pushing Angel out of it. "I'll give you the address," he bit out. "We'll meet there."

Her brows furrowed. "Oh. Okay."

"You'll like it."

She tilted her head to the side, studying him. "I'm sure I will."

He opened his mouth to explain himself because she seemed a little confused, and who wouldn't be with the way he said all the wrong things? But what came out was only, "See ya."

"See ya," she said and went back to her salad.

He turned and walked away, knowing when to shut up. He wasn't Mr. Feelings Talker like Angel. He headed toward the exit, a little shook up. Like he'd leaped and the chute had gotten all tangled up.

7
___________

Emily waited in the lobby of La Casa de Margarita, determined to get through to Jared. He was proving shockingly
difficult to seduce considering his reputation. She thought he
would've picked up her flirty cues days ago. What did she
have to do, get naked? She'd changed at work into a white V-
neck top that showed some cleavage, skinny jeans, and
spiked knee-high black leather boots. She left her hair down
and spritzed on some perfume that had hints of cinnamon
and vanilla, a potent male aphrodisiac according to the adver-
tisement. She was completely hookup ready right down to
her pale peach pushup bra and bikini panties. If he didn't get
it from her outfit and her flirty moves, she'd have to admit
defeat. It must mean he wasn't interested. Either that or he
was extremely dense. Maybe she should just put it out there.
Wear a sign with bright red letters—*ready for a fling*. Or *show
me a good time, please*. She smiled to herself and with some
kind of sixth sense turned her head and met his green eyes
from across the room just as he arrived.

He started toward her, wearing a navy blue close-fitting
sweatshirt that showed off his wide shoulders and faded
well-worn jeans. She met him halfway.

He looked behind her. "Where's Angel?"

"I didn't call him. I told you we're just friends." She leaned up on tiptoe and whispered in his ear, "I want you."

He pulled back. "Are you sure?"

"You're the good-time guy, right?" She looked up at him from under her lashes and lowered her voice to a seductive purr. "I want a good time."

His brows drew together. "No, you don't want the good-time guy. You need the good-for-you guy."

She threw her arms around his neck and kissed him both to shut him up and to get her point across that she really wanted *him*. Not Angel. His lips were firm and warm and not kissing her back. She started to pull away, embarrassed, but then he slid his hand into her hair and pulled her in for a hard, hungry kiss that sent her hopes soaring.

He pulled away so abruptly she nearly lost her balance. He steadied her with one hand on her arm, and their gazes locked for a long, sizzling moment.

"Jared, party of three," the host called. Obviously Jared had prepared for his stepbrother to join them.

"Just two," Emily called, holding up two fingers.

She laced her fingers with Jared's, and he let her. Progress. They followed the host to a table, where they were quickly given glasses of water, chips and salsa, and the drinks menu.

"Ooh, the margaritas are supposed to be fantastic here," she said.

"No drinks."

"Why not?"

He gave her a stern look. "Last time you drank you told me more than I needed to know."

That stung. She'd confided in him about her ex and what she'd been through. "I can drink if I want to."

"Not on my watch."

She scowled. "What happened to the good-time guy?"

"Hell if I know."

The waiter arrived and Jared ordered a virgin margarita for her. "See? That's fun too," he said after the waiter left.

"Seriously?" she asked in total exasperation.

"I can't handle you in my lap," he said, sounding kind of desperate.

"You think every time I drink I sit in a guy's lap?"

"Every time I've seen you drink, you sat in my lap."

"That was one time!"

He raised the menu in front of his face. "One time too many."

Geez. She couldn't believe how difficult it was to seduce this man. He'd kissed her back not five minutes ago! "If I'm so awful, then why're you here?"

He dropped the menu. "Because I wanted…I'm trying…I dunno." He scowled. "I'm just trying to do the right thing."

Tears sprang to her eyes. She couldn't even have a fun fling with the one man known for that.

She stood. "I'm sorry if I've made you uncomfortable. I just wanted a little fun."

He grabbed her wrist and held it. "Why me? Are you trying to hurt Angel?"

"No." She swallowed. "Everyone knows you're fun."

"And what happens after a little fun?"

"Nothing."

He released her wrist. "You deserve better than that. Don't settle for less. That's why Angel—ah!" He leaped out of his seat.

She'd dumped her glass of ice water over his head. She wasn't sorry either. "Don't say that name again."

He shook his head, and icy drops of water splashed her. "Turnabout is fair play," he said, snaking his arm around her waist and pulling her close.

"Oh," she breathed. He yanked her T-shirt forward and dropped a handful of dripping wet ice down the front of her shirt, making her yelp. Ice collided with her bra, lodging between her breasts, and slid down her stomach. She pulled away, shaking out her shirt and bra. Several people at nearby tables stared.

He smiled smugly. "Now we're even."

She narrowed her eyes. "I'm thinking you could use more ice."

The waiter returned in a hurry. "Can I take your order?"

She and Jared took one look at each other, still dripping wet, and burst out laughing. They *were* acting a little crazy for a restaurant.

She sat down. "We need a few minutes," she told the waiter.

Jared pulled off his sweatshirt and handed it to her. He had a black T-shirt on underneath. "You look chilly."

She glanced down. She had the wet T-shirt look, her nipples tight and pointing at him. "I'll be right back."

She headed to the restroom, took off the wet T-shirt and bra, and pulled on the sweatshirt still warm from his body. A little wet around the collar, but what could you do? She loved his scent still wrapped in his shirt—like apple pie and spice. She got a plastic take-out bag from the hostess and put her wet things in there before returning to the table and taking her seat.

"That's the second time you wore my sweatshirt," Jared said.

"So?"

He arched a brow. "I think you like wearing men's clothes."

"What's that supposed to mean?"

He smirked. "Maybe I need to buy more sweatshirts before you steal them all."

"I'm not stealing them. I'm borrowing them." She eyed his muscular arms now visible in the short sleeves and really wanted to see his chest too. The more Jared, the better. "Can I borrow that T-shirt?"

He leaned close, his voice husky. "Would you like me to eat lunch shirtless?"

"Yes, please."

He laughed.

"I'm serious."

His green eyes lit up. "I bet you are," he said on a laugh. She couldn't help but smile back.

The waiter returned to take their orders. Conversation flowed after that as she asked how Vince and Sophia were doing. Apparently Sophia was trying with little success to knit some baby booties, which she feared meant she was going to be a terrible mom. Vince, in return, dropped a bag of premade booties into her lap, which she didn't appreciate like he thought she would. They were a hoot. The food arrived, and they ate while she told Jared a little about her family—her extremely driven lawyer parents, her two older sisters with their perfect husbands and perfect children living in a wealthy suburb of Connecticut. Her sisters never missed an opportunity to brag about their super-devoted husbands who would never cheat.

"Ooh, you'll never guess what Steven did," Emily said, raising her voice to sound like her oldest sister, Claire. "He brought me wine after work and then rubbed my feet. He just knew I'd had a rough day with the kids." She rolled her eyes. "That's my Claire impersonation. She probably texted him and told him to do that. No man is that thoughtful."

Jared raised a brow.

She lifted a finger. "Here's Sara: Tim brings me breakfast in bed every morning. Then he makes me lunch and puts it in the fridge so I won't have to worry about lunch with the baby." She pursed her lips. "And guess what's in the lunch?"

Jared snorted. "What?"

"A love note. She puts them all in a scrapbook that she loves to show off."

Jared took a sip of water. "You don't get along with your sisters?"

She sighed. "I do. We're only a year apart, all three of us in a row, but…they're always rubbing it in my face that I'm the one that fell for a pretty face. Looks can only take you so far, they always say. About him, but also me. They call me the pretty one, Sara's the sweet one, Claire's the smart one." She blew out a breath. "Obviously I know looks aren't everything. My life has never been all sparkles and unicorns."

Jared looked behind her. "Spoke too soon. I just spotted a unicorn."

She grinned. "You're so easy to talk to. So nonjudgmental."

He spread his palms. "I'm pretty open-minded."

"Not that open-minded. You wouldn't let me drink."

"You'd probably fall asleep on me, and then I'd have to carry you out of here." One corner of his mouth lifted. "Please. Save me the embarrassment."

She laughed. "You want to come over after this? Or I could go to your place?"

He shook his head, suddenly serious. "I don't think that's a good idea."

"Why?" She grabbed her water glass and raised it threateningly. "And don't you dare say that name again! I'm warning you."

He inclined his head. "You love someone close to me."

She set her glass down. "I don't. Not anymore."

"Come on. Love doesn't just turn off like a faucet. I've seen it with my brothers. Once they fall—" he whistled and made a gesture like they dove off a cliff "—that's it. They're sunk." He stared at the table for a moment, his brow creased in concentration before he lifted his head and stared at her with a strange expression, almost like he'd suddenly remembered something.

"What is it?"

"Did the faucet turn off for you with…that guy we, uh, both know?"

"It's not like that for me at all. I don't love *that guy*, and I don't love my ex anymore. Maybe I never had true love." She found herself getting choked up. This was supposed to be a fun fling, and it was getting all screwed up. And now all she could think about was how she'd never had true love and she probably never would. She couldn't recognize the real thing, obviously.

Jared piped up. "Maybe you did have love, but—"

"So it's my fault?" she snapped.

He raised his palms. "Whoa, whoa, whoa. I didn't say that. You just had bad luck with your ex."

"And with Angel?"

"I thought we weren't supposed to say his name."

She glared at him.

"He's a great guy." He tapped the table. "That's just a fact." He met her eyes, something in them distant yet still locked on hers. His gaze turned heated. Her lips parted, and he turned away, breaking the connection.

She bit back a groan of frustration. She was never going to get through to him. So why did she want him more than ever?

He stood. "I gotta get going." He dropped some cash on the table. "Keep the sweatshirt," he added before he took off.

"I'll find another way to get excitement!" she called after him. "I'll do that jumping thing."

He stopped, shook his head, and kept going.

She lifted a finger for the waiter. "Margarita, please. Not a virgin."

Completely giving up on the excitement of a fling or freebase jumping (obviously neither one was going to happen, Jared was impossible and she wasn't crazy enough to try a jump without an experienced guide), Emily resigned herself to her normal, safe life focused on work, cooking, and reading. After lunch with Jared, she'd headed to Book It to find a nice juicy romance for vicarious excitement and spotted a flyer for a Thanksgiving cooking class taught by local chef Shane O'Hare. The class started the very next day. She called the number and managed to slip into the last available slot.

The following afternoon, she approached "the mansion" with great enthusiasm for her cooking class. The two-and-a-half-story white clapboard house was stunning with white columns on either side of the two-story portico and a wraparound porch. Its real name was the Ludbury House, and it was owned by the town of Clover Park. Community events were often hosted on the beautifully landscaped grounds, with the house itself reserved for weddings and the occasional fundraising dinner.

"Hello?" she called. The beautiful foyer with its crystal chandelier and grand staircase was empty. She peeked into an empty parlor room. She felt a little strange wandering around the place on her own.

A young woman with long, wavy strawberry blond hair, pale blue eyes, and a bright smile rushed out front. She wore a royal blue sheath dress with matching pumps. "Are you looking for the cooking class?"

"Yes."

"Right this way!" She turned on her high heels, with an enthusiastic wave of her hand. Emily followed her to the back of the house to a large professional-grade kitchen, where only one man stood in an apron.

"This is our instructor, Mr. O'Hare," the woman said.

"Shane," the man corrected. His cheeks flushed red just like his hair.

Emily smiled. "Yes, I recognize you from your ice-cream shop." Everyone in town knew Shane. He was thirtyish and married with four kids under four. Busy household, she imagined.

"And Something's Brewing Café too," the woman said. "Oh! Where are my manners?" She held out a hand and Emily shook it. "I'm Hailey Adams. The wedding planner for Ludbury House. Are you single?"

"Err...yes." She hadn't realized there was an official wedding planner associated with the house.

Hailey's blue eyes sparked with excitement. "I can help you with that!"

"No, that's not—"

"Down, girl!" a woman said on a laugh. Emily turned to see an older woman with white, spiky hair and an outfit that was very inappropriate for a woman well over sixty—a pink faux fur vest over a midriff-revealing red T-shirt with a heart on it that read Love. Her pink tutu was also patterned with hearts. She wore white tights and leopard-print Mary Janes. "You got to plan the weddings, not cause them to happen."

"Someone has to drum up business around here," Hailey replied, completely unfazed. "Oh! I think I hear another student." She rushed out of the room.

"Hey, Gran," Shane said.

"Hey, yourself." She went up on tiptoe to kiss Shane's cheek. Then she crossed to Emily, took her hand, and shook it in a surprisingly firm grip. "I'm Maggie O'Hare. Taught the boy everything I know, which is why I'm here to share some of my secret holiday recipes."

Emily smiled. "That sounds wonderful. I'm Emily."

Just then two more people arrived. Emily jolted, surprised to see Angel there. He walked in with a pretty young woman with shoulder-length brown hair. Though Angel didn't touch the woman, there was something protective about the way he walked with her, leading her to the center of the space.

"Shane," Angel said, giving him a pat-on-the-back bro hug, "Good to see you. I'm here under duress at Julia's request."

"Angel," Julia said softly, her cheeks flushing pink.

Angel turned to Julia and grinned his devilish, dimpled smile. She smiled back even as he said, "She needed someone who cooked worse than her so she wouldn't be embarrassed."

Julia mimed strangling him. He stuck out his tongue and rolled his eyes up like she'd succeeded.

Maggie introduced herself to Angel and Julia, who didn't smile during Maggie's friendly greeting. And then Angel introduced Julia to Emily and stepped back to talk to Shane.

Julia shook her hand, her grip weak despite the fact she wasn't petite. They were the same size, a hearty five foot seven. Up close, her brown eyes had a haunting sadness to them. "Nice to meet you," Julia murmured, her eyes already drifting away to Angel.

He reappeared by Julia's side and whispered something to her that seemed to make her relax.

Maggie rubbed her hands together. "Okay, now. Grab some aprons." She gestured to a row of hooks on the wall with a bunch of white aprons.

Emily went to get one. Angel got there first. He took one and handed it to Julia before taking one for himself. There was an easy way between the two of them that made Emily sure this was the woman Angel had said he loved. He'd never mentioned Julia by name, but his devotion to her was clear.

And the way Julia responded to him, only brightening under his attention, made her seem like a delicate flower in need of Angel's care. Seeing that, Emily was glad Angel had let her go. There couldn't have been a future for them with Julia in the picture.

They gathered around the large stainless steel prep table in the center of the room. Shane had just finished telling them about the sides they'd be preparing—his grandmother's corn-bread stuffing, Brussels sprouts with bacon dressing, and sweet potatoes in orange cups—when another student arrived.

Emily smiled. "Hi, Josh." This was a nice surprise. She'd never seen the friendly bartender outside of Garner's Sports Bar & Grill. He had a thick growth of stubble on his jaw like he hadn't shaved today, and his dark brown hair stuck up like he'd just rolled out of bed. The look really worked for him in a sexy and very appealing way. His black long-sleeve shirt hung loosely over ripped jeans.

Josh flashed a smile her way. "Hey, *you*, this forced class just got a whole lot better." She wondered if he even remembered her name with all the women he met at the bar. He crossed to her. "My boss insisted I show up here today and report back on the recipes for the restaurant." He lowered his voice conspiratorially. "I drew the short straw for the Sunday afternoon duty."

"Liar," Shane said with a grin. "You're a secret foodie."

Josh shot a warning finger at Shane that just made him laugh. Three middle-aged couples joined them, coming in together with the enthusiastic wedding planner Hailey.

Hailey wiggled her fingers at Josh. "Emily is single," she caroled.

Emily's cheeks burned.

"So am I," Josh caroled back.

Hailey grinned. "Looks like you too will have to pair up." She gestured for them to stand closer together.

Josh moved in and pressed flush against Emily's side. "Like this?"

Hailey beamed and gave him a thumbs-up before turning

and striding out of the room to do whatever it was she did on a Sunday afternoon at Ludbury House.

Josh turned to Emily with an infectious smile. "Is this good for you?"

Emily laughed and felt someone staring. She turned to find Angel watching her before quickly turning away.

"We do actually need everyone to pair up," Shane said. "That way everyone has a burner and a mixer."

"No problem," Josh said, bumping her with his hip. "We're good."

Angel and Julia were already paired up. Everyone else was a couple.

They began the cornbread stuffing with Maggie barking out orders and checking on each pair, correcting them as she moved around the room. "Really rip into that bread, Julia. Don't be afraid to tear it apart."

Julia nodded and tore the stale bread a little more forcefully. Angel made a growling face behind Maggie's back while he ripped into his piece of bread, making Julia bite her lip, holding back a laugh.

"Are you really a foodie?" Emily asked Josh while she watched him pick up a knife and slice the bread quickly into perfect rectangles.

He gestured to the pile of bread that he'd made short work of. "What do you think?"

"Have you thought about being a chef?" she asked.

"They don't tip the chef," he responded. "I clean up bartending."

She knew he did, especially on ladies' night. "Yes, but do you love bartending?"

"One day I'll have my own restaurant and bar," he said. "The whole deal."

"Pay attention, class!" Maggie barked like the general she'd suddenly become once class started. "Next we sauté the vegetables. Shane's chopped ahead of time, so gather your vegetables and to the stove!"

"She's scaring me," Josh whispered to Emily. She giggled.

"If you have something to say, you can tell the whole class," Maggie said, appearing in front of Josh and looking up at him. The petite badass general.

"Sorry, ma'am."

Maggie cackled. "I'm just *josh*ing with you." She elbowed him in the ribs. "Though I expect you to give me sex on the beach after this."

"She means the drink!" Josh said above the laughter of the whole class.

"Of course!" Maggie said. "I'm a happily married woman. Back to work!"

It was a really fun class for Emily between the hysterical Maggie and Josh flirting with her the whole time. She flirted back, unconcerned about him asking her out. She knew that was just his way. He flirted with her and every woman who walked into Garner's. She'd never have a fling with him because that would ruin ladies' night at her favorite bar. Totally awkward.

At the end of class, Shane invited them all to sign up for a onetime Christmas cooking class in a few weeks and asked them to remember his catering business for their next event. Emily added her name to the sign-up sheet for the next class along with everyone else. It had been a really fun, informative class.

"Toss your dirty aprons in the basket by the door," Maggie hollered above the chatter.

Emily started toward the door when the string on the back of her apron pulled tight. She glanced back over her shoulder. "Josh!"

He'd untied her. "What?" he asked, giving her his infectious smile that lit up his face. "I'm helping. Hey, you want to get a drink after this? On me."

"Sure, but I'll pay." She turned back and startled to find Jared standing in the doorway, glaring at her.

"I'll take her for drinks," Jared bit out.

She blinked. "How did you—"

"Let's go," Jared said.

"I'll meet you there," Josh said with a wink. "I owe someone sex on the beach."

Jared glared at Josh, took Emily's hand, and pulled her out of there.

"Wait," she said, breathless at his pace as he practically sprinted for the front door, "I need my jacket."

"I'll get it." Jared stalked back to the kitchen and returned a moment later. He held it out and helped her into it.

Garner's was just a couple blocks away, so she left her car behind and walked with Jared down the sidewalk. "How did you know I was here?" she asked.

"Angel texted me."

"Oh. Why?"

He stopped and pinned her with a hard look. "Why do you think?"

"I have no idea." *Please say it was to hook up with me.*

He cocked his head to the side. "Because someone had the bright idea of making you and Josh a couple." He resumed walking at a breakneck pace.

"So that bothered you?" she asked, a little giddy.

"Yes."

"Why?"

"Because."

"Because why?"

He didn't answer until they got to the door of the bar. "If anyone's going to give you sex on the beach, it's me."

She beamed at him. "Okay then!"

"After you." He opened the door and ushered her inside. The bar was crowded with people watching the Patriots football game. Jared found one empty bar stool and gestured for her to take it. He scanned the bar, probably looking for Josh, but he hadn't shown up yet.

She sat down, pleased with this turn of events. "I'm ordering a real margarita," she informed him. If he was going to go all caveman on her and pull her away from Josh, then he'd have to deal with her in all her alcohol-induced flirtiness.

He grinned, considerably less tense now that they were at

the bar and Josh was nowhere to be found. "A real margarita, huh? You looking to sit in my lap again?"

"Don't mind if I do." She hopped off the bar stool and gestured for him to take her place.

He did and then pulled her onto his lap, wrapping his arms around her from behind. He spoke in a low voice near her ear, bringing a rush of heat to her entire body. "I'm just holding you so you don't fall over when your drink puts you to sleep."

She snort-laughed. "That was only because I hadn't slept in days."

"Uh-huh. Likely story."

He gestured to the bartender, a woman with short fire-engine-red dyed hair, and ordered himself a beer and her a margarita. "So what's the deal with Josh?"

"No deal," she said.

"Angel said he was making the moves on you."

She laughed. "I had no idea Angel doubled as a spy." She turned sideways in his lap to look at him. "What do you care?"

He tapped the end of her nose. "Oh, I care. Sensible woman like yourself. Gotta look out for those so they don't get taken in by players."

"Hmmm…"

"What's that mean?"

"Nothing. I'm just humming."

He chuckled. "I was surprised to see Julia there."

"That's the woman Angel loves, isn't it?"

"Yup."

"Why aren't they together?"

"She's a grieving widow."

"Oh." That made a lot of sense, actually. She could feel the sadness radiating off of her. Emily was probably more in tune to that than most people due to her work in the oncology ward. Now that she'd seen the obvious devotion Angel had for Julia, she had to wonder why Jared pushed Angel to be with her. "Why did you try to get me and Angel back together?"

He stared at the bar. "I was trying to do the right thing. He was stuck and unhappy, and it didn't look like he'd ever move forward with her. I'm still not sure if he will. He regretted...he wondered if he'd made a mistake bailing on..." He met her eyes briefly and turned back to the bar. "Anyway, you said you loved him, and it seemed like I should just get out of the way."

She was about to ask more about Julia and why Angel couldn't move forward with her, but then their drinks arrived.

Jared paid and then held his beer bottle up by her margarita glass. "To sleep," he said, "since I'm sure this one drink is going to knock you out."

"Sure I always toast to sleep," she said on a laugh. She took a long swallow of delicious drink.

"I'm waiting," he said, still holding his glass up. "Don't leave me toast hanging."

"Oh." She clinked her glass against his. "To sleeping." She watched him take a sip of beer before adding, "Together."

He choked on his beer. She smiled and took another sip of margarita.

When he finally stopped sputtering, he set his beer down. "Proud of yourself? You nearly killed me."

She grinned. "I did not." She stopped smiling at the hot look in his eyes. She licked her lips.

"You want to get out of here?" he asked hoarsely.

"Yes," she said with no small amount of relief. Finally she was going to get her fling. She'd really given up all hope. She hopped off his lap.

"Let me just leave a tip." He pulled out his wallet.

She took a last sip of margarita before setting it back on the bar and froze when her gaze caught on the one TV that didn't have the game on. It was turned to the news.

And the news was her.

The volume was turned down, but it didn't matter, there was her ex-husband holding up a political campaign sign in his signature blue and red colors. Only this time, instead of his campaign slogan, it said, *Emily Maguire, will you remarry me?*

She swayed and nausea rose up in her throat. When would it end? The press would never leave her alone if Michael kept throwing her under the bus like this.

Jared waved a hand in front of her face. "Em? Ready to… oh, shit. What the hell?"

**8**

———

Emily pushed her way through the crowded bar and rushed to the ladies' room, where she promptly threw up in the toilet. She flushed, washed her hands, and grabbed a paper towel. She hated that Michael could still get to her like this. Seeing him in the news, pulling her into the spotlight, brought it all back. The utter humiliation of the sex scandal that she couldn't seem to get away from. She'd done nothing wrong, yet it made her look bad. And for Jared to see that was even worse. He was going to feel sorry for her. That was not sexy at all.

"Emily?" Jared called through the door. "You okay?"

"Give me a minute." She tossed the paper towel away.

"Okay."

She ran the water, cupped her hand, and swished her mouth out. Fortunately she was alone in the small two-stall bathroom. She took a deep, calming breath. There went her fun fling. It was like the universe didn't want her to ever have a good time. She looked in the mirror. Her skin was pale; her eyes watery. "Pull it together," she told herself.

She put on her game face, the one that said, *I'm having a pleasant time and everything is just fine*, before pulling open the door.

Jared took one look at her and wrapped her in a hug. "Are you okay?"

She let herself lean on his warm strength for a brief moment before straightening. "I, uh, I don't feel so well."

"I'll take you home."

She pulled away. "No, I got it. My car's only a couple blocks away."

"I'll walk over with you. My car's there too."

She knew he wouldn't take no for an answer, so she just headed to the exit. Jared fetched their coats and followed her. When they got outside, he handed her coat over, but she just held it. The crisp, cold air made her feel a little better.

They started walking back to the parking lot behind Ludbury House. After a few minutes of silence, Jared spoke up. "So what's the deal with your ex?"

"Nothing."

"He wants you back."

She said nothing. Who cared if Michael wanted her back? She'd never go back to him.

"Do you want him back too?"

"Don't ask me that," she snapped. Honestly, Jared knew how awful Michael was to her. How could he think for one minute she'd even consider it?

"Want me to tell him to get lost?" he asked.

She blew out a breath. "No."

He tried to hold her hand, but she busied herself putting her coat on and then stuffed her hands in her pockets. She wasn't up to flirting or anything remotely close to lust. She felt dirty all over again. Michael's filth covered her.

When they got to the parking lot, Jared stopped and studied her for a moment. "You want me to come over? I've been told I'm pretty easy to talk to."

She'd said that to him over their lunch before, but now she wanted nothing more than to burrow back to the comfort of her home. She shook her head.

"Em, I'm a little worried about you. You seem shaken up."

"Don't pity me," she said. "It's over." But, of course, it was never truly over. Michael wouldn't let it be.

He backed away. "Yeah. Okay. Well, goodnight." And with that, he strode toward his truck and took off.

She stared after him, suddenly realizing he might've taken that the wrong way. Her mind was on Michael. She hadn't meant it was over with him. Oh, what did it matter? Her night was ruined.

She drove home, cursing Michael the whole way, headed toward her assigned parking spot only to discover what appeared to be Michael standing there with roses and a camera crew. A news van was parked nearby. She slammed on the brakes and made a quick turn into another parking area around the corner of the building, her heart racing.

Damn him. He brought them to her door. He probably proposed to her there too.

She was so angry, she was shaking as she pulled her cell phone from her purse. She punched in the number that was still in her phone from when he'd called her before.

He answered in a pleasant tone. "Hello, Emily, where are you?"

"The answer is no," she said. "And if you don't leave my apartment complex, I will call the cops."

"Are you here? I'm standing on public property."

She closed her eyes, trying to think. What was the fastest way to get rid of him? "Michael, I swear to God, I will get a restraining order against you, which will be public knowledge. Would you like everyone to know you're a deranged stalker? Because I'll make sure that's exactly what they think."

"Fine, I'll leave. *For now.*"

"For good!" she shouted into the phone, but he'd hung up.

She turned the car around so she could see exactly when Michael and the news van left. Finally, a good half hour later, they left.

She pulled into her assigned parking spot and managed to get into her apartment before she broke down in tears. And then suddenly she was furious that he could still get to her like that, especially after she'd actually started to enjoy herself today. She grabbed the framed picture off the end table of her family last Christmas with her perfect sisters smiling with their perfect husbands and threw it against the wall.

The glass shattered.

"Fucking sicko!" she screamed before sinking to the floor in a tight ball and wrapping her arms around her knees. She'd never be free of him.

Jared helped himself to a slice of pumpkin pie at the kitchen island in his brother Gabe's large gourmet kitchen. It was Thanksgiving, and he marveled at how their already large family had grown. The dining room table fit twelve of them, and they'd cleared the living room furniture for another long table. Not only were four of his five brothers married, but they'd also brought along some of their wives' families. The wall between the living room and dining room had separated them for dinner, but dessert was buffet style in the kitchen.

Angel appeared at his side and helped himself to a slice of pumpkin pie. "How's Emily?"

"Fine." He shoved a big piece of pie in his mouth, not wanting to talk about the woman they'd both lusted for. She'd told him it was over, so whatever bit of flirty fun they'd had was done. And after seeing her reaction to her ex proposing on the news, it was clear she was still reeling from the hell her ex had put her through.

"How'd things go after class?" Angel asked, adding some whipped cream in a big swirl to his pie.

"How'd things go for you and Julia after class?"

"Fuck you."

"Are they fighting again?" his smartass older brother Luke asked. He was way into money, his job was wealth management, and he probably wanted to get in on another round of betting.

A low murmur began among his brothers, and then conversation died as everyone turned to see what would happen next between Jared and Angel.

"Nothing to see here, folks," Jared announced. "Go back

to stuffing your faces." He took another forkful of pie, and Angel did the same.

Conversation resumed.

"Julia and I are just friends," Angel said in a low voice.

"So are me and Emily."

Angel raised his brows. "Why? Don't you think she's sexy?" He elbowed him in the gut.

Jared bristled. "Her ex proposed to her on the news, and then she ran to the bathroom. I assume she puked, because she was pale and shaky after that."

Angel's brown eyes went wide. "Really? I missed that. What an asshole." He shook his head. "He should just fucking leave her alone."

Jared grunted.

Angel dug into his pie, and after a moment, he added, "Still, that doesn't mean you can't be with her."

"She doesn't want that. She—"

*Ding. Ding. Ding.*

Nico was clinking a spoon against a glass to get everyone's attention. The room fell silent. Nico wrapped an arm around his wife Lily's shoulders and pulled her close. He beamed. "We have an announcement."

"I'm pregnant!" Lily exclaimed.

"Congratulations!" their mom exclaimed, rushing over to hug Lily.

"Salute!" their stepdad said, raising his glass. Everyone raised their glass with a chorus of cheers and congratulations.

"The Spencer dynasty continues!" Lily's dad said. He was an extremely wealthy, extremely imposing man in a tweed sports jacket.

"Marino dynasty," Nico corrected. "C'mere and give your grandchild your Spencer blessing."

Lily's dad quickly worked his way to Lily and then just stood there, seeming unsure what to say.

Lily hugged him. "Thanks, Dad."

"Thank you," he said in a gravelly voice; then he shook Nico's hand in a formal congratulation before stepping back.

"How far along?" Vince boomed.

Lily laughed. "Nine weeks. I got pregnant on our honeymoon, but we didn't want to say anything at first. We just wanted you and Sophia to enjoy the attention."

"Nine weeks?" Sophia asked. "No morning sickness?"

"Nope!" Lily said with a smile. "I feel great. Guess I'm just lucky."

Sophia glared daggers at her, prompting Lily to quickly add, "I'm sure I'll get all that the second time around."

Sophia pursed her lips. "I'm sure." Poor Sophia had only had small bites of plain bread at their feast. Lily had piled everything on her plate.

Everyone gathered in close to Lily and thumped Nico on the back, congratulating him. Jared felt a strange empty ache as his family rejoiced. His brothers were moving on to families of their own. His life was standing still.

He turned to Angel, who was staring at the floor, a pained expression on his face.

"You okay?" Jared asked.

Angel's head snapped up, and he forced a smile that didn't fool Jared for a second. "Yeah. Great news, huh?"

"Yeah." Angel's life wasn't just standing still, it was stuck. He didn't know the right thing to do for Angel. On the one hand, it was unlikely the faucet of love would turn off for him with Julia. He'd realized that recently. His brothers fell and fell hard. But if that love would never be returned, shouldn't Angel at least try to find someone who would love him back? Was there really only one person out there for Angel?

And then it hit him. What if there was only one person out there for Jared too? What if that one person was Emily? He wanted her more than he'd ever wanted anyone. That wasn't going away. If anything, it was getting worse. He couldn't stop thinking about her. But she'd said it was over. She had an ex proposing to her again. Not that she wanted her ex back, but he got the feeling she wasn't looking for anything more than a good time, with all her baggage. It felt like karma, this role reversal where he was on the receiving end of a casual encounter. He wasn't sure how to move forward with her, wasn't sure if that was even an option.

It seemed that he and Angel were both stuck.

Two days later, Jared showed up for his Saturday morning Captain Huddle duty with no clear plan other than a step forward. He wanted Emily to know he was interested, but didn't want to rush to the bedroom. She meant more to him than that. Yes, that was what he'd do. He gave himself a mental pat on the back for that brilliant idea. He was looking for more than a good time, and if by some freak chance she was too (despite his gut feeling to the contrary), maybe they'd have something…real good.

Delusional thinking, that was all he had left in his pitiful arsenal.

"Hi, Jared," Emily said with a big smile as she handed him the goody bag.

He was instantly relieved to see her looking happy again. "Hey. How're you doing after, you know, that thing with—"

"I'm fine. I took care of the problem." She beamed. "And I'm ready for excitement and fun."

He studied her for a moment, unsure what that meant. Just a blanket statement? She wasn't giving him any kind of signal that he could read. "Oh, yeah?"

"Yeah."

"Like what?"

She put a hand on his arm and his hopes rose, along with an important body part, as she went up on tiptoe to whisper, "I'm going free jumping."

He scowled. She was deliberately antagonizing him with this shit. He pushed his eye mask up to glower at her. "It's free*base* jumping, not free jumping, and I told you you're not doing that."

She lifted one shoulder. "I can if I want."

He ground his teeth and slammed the eye mask back in place. "After your shift, we're going to the mall."

"We are?"

"Yeah. You can do the bungee jump there." The Eastman

mall had recently set up a bungee trampoline. You could jump as high as the second floor all while safely attached to a harness tethered to multiple bungee cords. That was both exciting and fun.

A big smile spread across her face. "Awesome!"

He grunted. She smiled some more, twirling a long lock of glossy brown hair.

He turned and headed for Chris's room, unexpectedly smiling.

Four hours later, on the drive to the mall, Jared was still smiling because Emily was bubbling with excitement over her first bungee jump. Also, she'd changed out of her scrubs and into a sweater and jeans that showed off an hourglass figure with a narrow waist and curvy hips. She'd added some perfume with hints of cinnamon and vanilla that made him want to lick her all over. *Down, boy.*

He parked the truck and took in her sparkling brown eyes and flushed cheeks with a bemused smile. "Ready?" he asked.

"Let's go!" She hopped out of his truck, and he led the way to the wing of the mall where they'd set up the bungee trampoline. There was a kid on it flying through the air, bounding up again, and doing somersaults. It looked like a lot of fun. And very safe with several bungee ropes, a harness, and that huge trampoline to land on. He'd never cared so much about safety until he met Emily. He hoped he wasn't losing his edge. Nah. He was still a risk-taking adrenaline junkie. Someone had to look out for Emily, that was all. The woman was on the hunt for excitement. He just happened to be the one close at hand.

"You're next," he said, helping her out of her jacket.

She frowned. "This isn't a bungee jump. It's just a trampoline." She pointed accusingly. "There's a kid on it. He can't be more than eight years old!"

"What'd you think, I was going to let you leap off the roof of the mall?"

She crossed her arms. "You said it was exciting. This is for kids."

"Adults can go on it too. Besides, look how high you can jump. This isn't a regular old trampoline. It's supercharged."

She looked at the trampoline skeptically. "Are you going on it too?"

"Nah. I don't need any more excitement." All of his energy had to go toward reeling in his lust for her.

"What kind of excitement are you getting?"

"Plenty." *Not really.*

She pursed her lips in a sexy pout.

He bit back a groan. "Don't do that."

"What?" she asked, her brown eyes sparkling mischievously.

"Get in line, missy," he said. "You're up next."

She sauntered over to the entrance of the attraction, working those hips. She stopped and looked at him over her shoulder with a smile. He shook his head. She knew what she was doing to him. This getting-to-know-you stuff without the getting-to-touch-you stuff took self-restraint to the level of extreme sport.

No one else was waiting in line, so a few minutes later Emily took off her sneakers and was strapped in. She started at a small jump, hardly going anywhere.

"Higher!" he hollered. "Push off."

She did. "Ah!" she yelped as she flew up really high, nearly to the second floor.

He grinned. "More. Do a flip!"

She raised her arms as she jumped. "I don't know how to do a flip!" she hollered back.

"Try!"

She leaped a while more, getting higher and higher, squealing and laughing. It looked like a ton of fun. Then she tucked and managed a somersault before landing. "I did it!" she hollered, jumping some more.

The guy running it announced her time was up and pulled her back down with the bungee cords. She stepped out of the harness and threw herself unexpectedly in Jared's arms, making him stagger back.

She smiled up at him, flushed and happy. "That was so fun! Do you think it was as exciting as free jumping?"

His lips twitched. "More."

She glanced at his mouth and then met his eyes. He stifled a groan and stepped out of her embrace. He couldn't take things slow if she kept throwing herself at him. "Let's get lunch at the food court."

This was the absolute last time he would be alone with her, he promised himself as they stood in line for pizza. He could only take so much temptation. He'd keep it to texts and phone calls for a while so they could get to know each other better. If he gave in to lust, she'd be out the door before he got any words out about feelings stuff. Maybe he should ask Mr. Feelings Talker to write him a script to follow. No, that was too weird given Angel and Emily's history.

Luckily next weekend he was heading up to Vermont for a ski weekend with Angel. They went every year the first weekend of December. They both loved the rush of the black diamond slopes. Maybe he could figure out a way to get some advice on the long drive without coming right out and admitting he needed help with a woman. A hypothetical situation for a friend. Yeah, that could work.

They settled at a table in the food court with slices of pepperoni pizza and bottled water. They dug into their food and ate in companionable silence. The mall speakers were already blaring Christmas carols. The cheerful *"Feliz Navidad"* added a festive note to their lunch date. Was it a date? He hadn't actually asked her out. More like told her they were doing this. His head was starting to hurt. It was damn difficult to move things to the next level with their clothes on.

Emily took a sip of water. "We should go skydiving next."

He stiffened. She wouldn't be doing anything that dangerous on his watch. He ignored the fact that he'd gone skydiving on plenty of occasions. This was exactly why he needed to bubble wrap her. She was hell bent on adventure, and he couldn't bear the thought of her getting hurt in any way. "You're not ready."

"Of course I am! I just bungee jumped."

"That was a trampoline."

She smacked his arm. "I told you that wasn't a real bungee jump."

"You know what's real exciting? Porn."

"Okay, let's do that."

"I was kidding!"

She leaned in, smiling her seductive smile. "You're pushing me to extreme measures."

He leaned back. "I'm not pushing you to anything!"

She lowered her voice. "You know how long it's been since I've had sex?"

"Yes. You told me when you were passed out on my sofa. I quizzed you and you mumbled all your secrets."

"I did not!" She paused, her brows scrunched down. "Wait, did I?"

He chuckled. "I also know the last time you flipped your mattress, that you're overdue for a physical, and your favorite toothpaste." Not really, but she was fun to tease.

"Ha! When was the last time you had sex?"

He went back to his pizza. He hadn't been with anyone since he met her. That fact was too embarrassing to admit. She'd think he was pining for her. Which he was.

"Well?" she pressed.

"Eat your pizza."

She smirked and took a bite of pizza. After she chewed, she said, "Dr. One-and-Done is a prude! I never would've guessed."

He set down his pizza. "That's it."

She wiggled her fingers at him. "Ooh, what're you going to do? Wave bye-bye? That's what you do. Run and hide, hunk-a-nator."

He snorted. "I can't decide if I'm mad at you or about to laugh."

She leaned across the table. "Kiss me."

"Em—"

She grabbed him by the collar, hauled him close and kissed him. He reacted without thought, sliding his hand into her silky hair, deepening the kiss. She tasted a little spicy like pizza and also intoxicating Emily. He needed to get closer, feel more of her pressed against more of him. Someone hollered, "Go for it, man!" He pulled away.

They went back to their lunch. Her lips curled into a small smirky smile of triumph. He was torn between bolting and grabbing her for more. *Cool it.*

"You done?" he asked after they'd both finished their slice. He stood with his tray.

"Yup," she said.

They tossed the trash and headed for the exit in silence. His only thought was that he had to get her home and away from him. Keeping his hands off was too much to ask any man in serious like/lust.

He stopped at the passenger-side door of his truck, unlocked it, and opened it for her. She threw her arms around his neck and kissed him again. He couldn't help himself. He dove into sweet insanity. She tasted amazing, she smelled amazing, she felt amazing. He lost control. The kiss got hot and heavy real fast, right there in the mall parking lot. He pulled away first, resting his forehead against hers, breathing hard and trying to get control again. "Emily, I'm—"

Her fingers covered his lips. "Shh, don't say anything. Just let it be."

They slammed together again.

"Come to my place," she said against his mouth, kissing him again. "Please."

"Yes, okay."

She beamed. "Okay!"

He drove her back to her apartment in Clover Park, but by the time he got there, he was having second thoughts. What if she thought one fun time was enough? What if he was the one left behind? He hadn't worked up a game plan yet, and he couldn't afford to fumble this.

He walked her to her door and gave her a chaste kiss on the forehead. "Bye, Emily."

"Bye! After all that kissing?" She put her hands on her hips. "Come on!"

He stepped back. "Sorry. It's just—"

She held up a hand. "You know what? Fine! Obviously it's never going to happen!"

"What're you so mad about? I'm just being a good guy."

She threw up her hands. "I can't believe I got the one player who won't play!"

"Sorry to disappoint you!" he barked as too much emotion and lust tangled up, messing with his head. "You can stop *accidentally* running into me in the cafeteria."

"I haven't run into you in the cafeteria in a week! Argh!" She went inside and slammed the door.

He wanted to kick something, and, at the same time, he wanted to barge into her apartment and finish what they started. She was making him insane.

He drove straight to Angel's place. He was the only one who could help him with this bizarre situation. Angel did this kind of thing for a living, untangling emotion and turning it into a plan. He was dimly aware that he was bringing the woman they'd both lusted over between them again and that it was wrong to rub Angel's face in it, given he was so stuck with Julia, and how Emily used to love him, but all Jared cared about was getting a game plan. He couldn't live like this, not knowing what to do, fighting his own lusty instincts.

"What's the matter?" Angel asked when he opened the door. "You look crazed."

He stepped inside. "I feel crazed. I kissed Emily, all right? More than once." He shoved both hands in his hair. "I screwed up."

"How did you screw up?"

Jared fumbled around for how to explain. He really, really liked her. He really, really lusted for her. He really, really didn't want to be the one left behind.

"Did you sleep with her?" Angel asked.

Jared was quiet because he nearly had.

"You have my blessing," Angel said like the saintly priest he was. *Dammit.*

"I don't need your blessing!" He shoved Angel, and Angel shoved him back. "You know, I'm really sick of this whole saintly thing you've got going on! You say you're not a saint, but you act like it, going around blessing people to sleep with the woman who fell in love with you." He raised a hand to slap Angel, but his brother moved quick, blocking him.

"Hey, cool it," Angel snapped.

"Stop being a damned saint."

Angel shook his head. "She's all yours, Dr. Bozo."

His gut churned. He wished he never knew that Emily had loved Angel. After her history in the love department, she just wanted some fun. He didn't know how to move things to where he wanted them, and that pissed him off because Angel knew the secret to getting Emily there and he didn't.

"You want to talk?" Angel asked.

"How did you...what did you..." He raked a hand through his hair. "Never mind. It's stupid."

"Give her a chance." Angel socked his arm a little harder than usual. Jared rubbed the spot. "What're you afraid will happen?"

He started pacing the living room. "Nothing. I'm not afraid of anything. And nothing's going to happen."

"But it already did. You kissed her more than once."

Jared stopped pacing and glared at Angel. "Shut up, idiot. You have no clue what I'm up against here."

"You're a little freaked because you actually feel something for her." Angel raised his brows. "Maybe something a little deeper than your usual hookup."

Jared couldn't bring himself to say it out loud. The thought that ran in circles around his head. What if Emily just wanted him for one fun time? Or worse, what if Jared ended up hurting her?

"Only one way to find out," Angel said like he was a damned mind reader.

Jared slammed his hands on his hips. "How do you know what I'm thinking?"

"Social worker training. All I do is listen, listen, listen." He raised a finger. "To what's being said and *not* said."

"How can you know what's not said!" Jared exclaimed.

Angel ignored that. "And I know you probably as well as I

know myself. You're afraid of what *might* happen, but there's only one way to find out what *will* happen."

He stopped pacing as his gut churned over all the many ways this could go wrong. The stakes felt too high.

He held up a hand. "I can't do this."

"So don't," Angel said.

"You'd like that, wouldn't you?" he snarled. It didn't matter that Angel loved Julia. He'd been with Emily, and that still pissed Jared off. More so because Jared hadn't been, and for a good cause, a real relation—was that what he wanted? A relation—he couldn't even think the word when it came to actually having one. *Man up!* Okay, yes. That was what he wanted. A relation—more than a good time. Who was he kidding? He couldn't even think the word. Maybe he *was* just the good-time guy. And maybe that meant sticking to women who didn't cause so much emotion that he couldn't think straight.

Angel studied him for a minute. "I want you to be happy, bro. Grab a little happiness for me, wouldja?"

"See? This is why I tried to give Emily to you before. I knew you weren't happy." He sucked in air and blurted, "Do you think there's just one person out there for you?"

"Yes," Angel said quietly.

"But then…" He didn't want to say Angel was fucked, but he clearly was.

"I know," Angel said, meeting his eyes unflinchingly. "I wish I could let go of Julia, but I can't."

Jared shook his head in silent commiseration.

Angel slapped him on the back. "It'll be good to get away next weekend. Beer?"

Jared felt a weight lift from his shoulders. He really needed this annual ski weekend. "Yeah. Can't wait. Let's watch the game."

He didn't have to be tempted next Saturday because he wouldn't be doing his usual visit to the pediatric ward. By the time he got back, surely he'd have a good game plan. Yes, this was just what he needed—the cold, crisp air, skiing the black diamonds, and some excitement that did not involve the woman who made him crazed.

But as he settled on the sofa, he couldn't focus on the game. All he could think about was her soft lips, her scent, her curves that fit against him perfectly. *Stop it.* He shifted uncomfortably and took a long pull on his beer. *Just focus on the game.*

He glanced at Angel, who jerked his chin at him. "Good game, huh? Close one."

"Yeah."

Next weekend would be easier. Just two bros and no chicks.

## 9

Jared whistled as he headed outside early on Saturday morning, skis and gear in hand to load into the bed of his pickup truck. Angel would show up at any minute, and then they were off. Vince said he'd step in for the Captain Huddle visit while Jared was away. Vince had roped their mom into Sophia-babysitting duty (literally babysitting, he wanted someone to watch out for the baby and make sure Sophia didn't starve him). Unfortunately, the two women had no plans to sit quietly at home as Vince had instructed, but instead planned a trip to the mall for maternity clothes. Jared knew all this because Vince had bitched about it over the phone last night, hoping Jared would give some medical advice that kept Sophia home. No can do.

Angel honked the horn as he pulled up, and Jared lifted a hand. But then two people got out of the car—Angel and Emily. *Fuck.* What did Angel do? He was screwing everything up. Jared didn't have a game plan yet. Hadn't figured out the right words. He was supposed to casually get advice from Angel on the drive up for his hypothetical friend. He wasn't ready to be thrown into the deep end.

"Hi, Em," Jared said in a surprisingly calm voice given he wanted to shake his stepbrother. "Angel, can I talk to you for a minute?"

"Go," Angel said to Emily.

"Hi!" Emily said with a bright smile as she passed him before heading over to his truck and settling into the cab.

"She's all yours for the weekend," Angel said as he put Emily's wheeled suitcase into the flat bed of Jared's truck.

Jared stomped over to Angel. "What the hell are you doing?"

Angel smiled serenely. "I told her, let's see, what were my exact words? 'Want to go skiing with Jared for a weekend in Vermont?'" He socked him on the shoulder. "Give you one guess what she said. And I know about Captain Cuddle. I'm doing it this weekend."

"Vince told you?"

"Yeah, he couldn't bear to leave Sophia. He's going maternity clothes shopping with her and Mom."

"Whipped," Jared muttered.

"No kidding," Angel said. "Have fun. Don't come back a virgin."

Jared snorted. "You know you crossed a line, butting in here. I'm thinking payback."

"It's for your own good, Dr. Bozo." Angel slapped him on the back, turned, and left.

Jared took a deep breath and returned to his truck. He got in the driver's side and looked over at Emily. "You ever ski black diamonds?"

"Just bunny slope," she said, "but I'm eager to move on to something more exciting." She slowly licked her lips in an extremely suggestive way.

"Why does everything out of your mouth sound like a proposition?"

"Because you're used to getting propositions?"

"What about your ex?" *What's your emotional baggage on a scale of one to ten? Do you want me for more than my body?*

She frowned. "What about him?"

He opened his mouth and shut it again. "Never mind." He watched Angel pull away and then turned back to her and blurted, "Are you over Angel?"

She made a weird growling noise. "If I had ice water, I'd

dump it on you again! How many different ways can I say I want you?"

He cupped the back of her neck, pulled her in, and kissed her deeply, a carnal promise of more. She moaned in the back of her throat, her fingers clutching his jacket. He kissed her for a long time until he was finally forced to pull away because his body was urging him to do more than he could in the confines of the truck. Her lips were pink, her brown eyes bright. She smiled, grabbed him by the jacket and pulled him back in for more. She finally let him up for air just as he was considering dragging her into his lap. He had to slow things down. They needed to talk about stuff.

"Emily—"

"I'm so turned on right now."

He jammed a hand in his hair. "I'm not sure what you think this weekend is, but—"

"It's a onetime, fun time, right?"

He started the truck. "We're not spending the weekend. Just a day trip." He couldn't spend the whole weekend with her and say goodbye. He'd ski with her, kiss her, and then say goodbye. He was never going to be able to live up to her one-and-done expectation. He wanted her too much. He *liked* her too much.

She blew out a noisy breath. "Whatever." Then she muttered, "Big 'fraidy cat."

He pulled out into the road and hit the accelerator. "I'll show you 'fraidy cat. I'm gonna dominate those black diamonds."

She sighed.

"Don't you have to work today?" he asked.

"I usually do. This is the first Saturday I've had off in two years. It seemed like a good opportunity for fun."

"It will be fun."

She fiddled with the radio, looking for a station. "I used to have a lot more fun in my life. I loved coasters and driving fast and parties, meeting new people."

"Yeah? Me too."

She found a Christmas carol station and left it there on

Bing Crosby's "I'll Be Home for Christmas." It made the cab feel cozy and intimate. Her cinnamon and vanilla scent wafted over him, making him ravenous. For her.

She went on. "Then I sort of shrank my little world until I felt like I couldn't breathe anymore." She blew out a breath. "I really thought someone like you would be more open to having a good time."

"I'm very fun. We'll have a good time."

"We'd better or I want my money back."

He glanced over at her. "What money?"

"I paid Angel for his half of the room."

"What? He would've let you have it for free. I'll pay for your half of the room."

"So we *are* spending the night."

He eyed her. "Emily—"

"One night. I need to find the old fun Emily again. If you're not up for it, I guess I'll find someone—"

"One night." She was *not* going to be finding some random hookup.

"Thank you."

He glanced over at her with that catlike smile of satisfaction and felt a surge of raw desire. Okay, one night. Then they'd talk about stuff. Maybe taking the edge off his lust would help him think clearer. She had to understand this wasn't just a hookup for him. She might've gotten the wrong impression because of his rep.

Except the more time he spent with her, the more his gut feeling was confirmed—he was the one looking for a commitment, and she was the one just in it for a good time.

Emily loved the view on the ski lift and the company. Though she had to admit, she was a little worse for the wear. The day started out so promising when she perched on top of her first ski run of the day. Half an hour later, she was bumped and bruised after falling on her ass too many times to count.

Jared rode the ski lift next to her, his arm and leg pressed snugly against hers. She wasn't sure if that was intentional or not, but she liked it. She was ready to get hot cocoa and sit in the lodge the rest of the day, but she felt kinda bad for him. They still hadn't made it past the bunny slope.

They got off the lift, and she faced the small hill with grim determination. Then she just stood there, frozen in place, unwilling to risk more falling on her ass.

Jared appeared at her side. "I thought you said you did bunny slope before."

"I did."

"When?"

"When I was, uh, twelve."

"So, it's been…how many years?"

*Eighteen years, but who's counting?*

"I'm going to get it soon." She pushed off and headed straight down, picking up speed faster and faster; then she remembered Jared said she should keep her knees apart at a slight angle. She tried to do that and started to wobble. Jared swerved expertly in front of her and held her up, skiing backwards down the hill, guiding her down with him.

"Thanks!" she said breathlessly. Skiing was a lot more fun when she wasn't falling on her ass.

"You got it," he said. He glanced over his shoulder at the terrain and maneuvered her safely to the bottom of the hill. "Want to go again?"

"Yeah, it's fun when you're keeping me upright."

They did several more trips down the hill like that. She was having fun, but she had to wonder what Jared was missing out on. "It's not very exciting for you," she said when they reached the bottom of the hill. "If you want to go on some black diamond runs, I don't mind. I'll just hang out in the lodge and drink hot cocoa."

"Hey, you paid for an exciting ski weekend and that's exactly what you're going to get. Come on. We're almost ready for Jane's Intermediate Hill." He grinned.

They got on the ski lift, and she looked over at Jane's Intermediate Hill that had a bunch of little kids skiing like demons down it. "You really think I'm ready?" she asked. "They're going so fast. It must be a higher slope."

"No." He laughed. "You show no signs of improving, but it's fun to ski down with you."

She gave him a quick kiss. He gazed into her eyes and kissed her back. The hard press of his lips felt so good she almost missed their stop. He pulled her off and set her straight toward Bunny One.

"Maybe I can move to Bunny Two by the end of the day," she said halfheartedly.

"Maybe," he allowed. "Let's see how you do when you don't have me to hang onto."

Her butt hurt a lot. "I like hanging onto you."

"Then we'll stay on Bunny One."

By sunset, Emily was exhausted and ready to warm up in the lodge. Jared agreed though she knew this wasn't the exciting ski weekend he'd envisioned with Angel. Hopefully, she could make it up to him later. They settled side by side into overstuffed chairs with steaming mugs of hot cocoa in front of a roaring fire.

"I heard the hotel has several nice restaurants," she said. "I looked it up online."

Jared stared into the fire. "Maybe we should head back."

Her jaw dropped. "It's a five-hour drive!"

He kept staring at the fire. "All the more reason to get a move on. We can grab a bite at a rest area on the way home."

She lowered her voice. "Are you…not attracted to me?"

His gaze snapped to hers. "Come on. You know it's not that."

"Do you know what this night could mean to me?" she whispered. "It would help me finally move on."

He narrowed his green eyes. "Move on from what exactly?"

"From the scandal. I want to know I can still have fun with a man without commitment."

He was quiet for so long she wondered if she'd said the wrong thing.

"What if I don't want you to move on?" he asked, gazing into the fire.

"What do you mean? You're actually looking for a relationship? Dr. One-and-Done?"

"Forget it," he muttered.

She put a hand on his arm. "I'm sorry. Did I misunderstand? I thought…well, I thought this is what you do. Hook up with nurses on the weekend in the service of Venus?"

He set his jaw and met her eyes with a hard look. "That's right. So let's get to it."

She hopped up, excitement humming through her. "Okay then! Let's go!"

They made the short ten-minute drive to the hotel and checked in. But when they got to the room, Jared didn't do anything. He just sat on the end of the queen-sized bed, elbows resting on his knees, looking at the floor. She really hoped he wasn't still holding back because of Angel. She was so over him.

She dropped to her knees in front of him, wrapped her arms around his waist, and kissed him. He groaned and pulled her up, standing with her, and then kissed her like his life depended on it. Urgent, hot, deep kisses that were completely unlike any kisses they'd had before. Her knees went weak and she clung to him, her fingers gripping his wide shoulders. He palmed her ass and ground her against him as he kissed her senseless. He pulled back only long enough to pull her sweater over her head and then expertly flicked open the front clasp of her bra.

"Gorgeous," he murmured, gazing at her breasts before claiming her mouth again, his hot tongue thrusting inside as his hands palmed her breasts. He rolled and tugged her hard nipples, causing an aching, throbbing need lower where she desperately needed his touch. He slipped the bra straps from her shoulders and tossed it to the side.

"Jared," she said on a moan, tugging at his shirt, running her hands under it, reveling in the heat and strength of his rippling back muscles as he leaned down to capture one aching nipple in his mouth. He used his tongue and teeth on the rigid point and she slid a hand into his hair, holding him there.

"So good," he murmured before shifting to her other breast, bending her back over his arm so she could do nothing but cling to him as his tongue rasped over her, and then he took her in more fully, suckling hard, making her ache.

He lifted his head and captured her mouth again in a rush of possession as his thick muscled leg wedged between hers. She was lost in sensation, already hot and wet and ready.

She tore her mouth from his. "Take me," she half begged, half demanded.

He didn't need any more encouragement than that. He undid her jeans and yanked them down, her panties followed, and he slid his fingers into her hot, wet folds as he kissed her again. She fumbled for the button on his jeans, her fingers trembling as he stroked her and then thrust his fingers inside. It had been so long, too long. She whimpered as her knees went weak.

He released her mouth and trailed hot kisses along her jaw down the side of her neck before letting her go long enough to turn her in his arms so her back was to his front. He cupped her breast in one large hand as he kissed the side of her neck and up to her ear, his tongue running along the sensitive shell.

"Jared, get naked." She tried to turn in his arms, but he snaked his other arm around her waist and held her in place.

His words ran hot over her skin. "I want to play with you first. If I only get one time, it's gotta last." He was referring to his Dr. One-and-Done status, but suddenly she wanted a lot more than once.

"You can have…" She trailed off as his hand delved between her legs. Her head fell back against his shoulder as the sensations overwhelmed her. He was shockingly in tune with her as he played with her, his other hand caressing her breast. He stroked firmly and then lightly, then in teasing circles while she panted breathlessly until all of the sensation centered on that one spot made her breath catch as she climbed, aching and rocking with his rhythm, right to the edge of release. He stilled his hand and held her firmly. She grabbed his arm, trying to make him move, but he merely chuckled.

He nipped the side of her neck. "You're a lot of fun." Then he dropped his arms from her body.

She turned to face him, torn between frustration and a desperate need for more. She grabbed for his shirt and peeled it off him, taking in golden skin and muscles defined she was sure from the physical work he enjoyed. She ran her hands over his chest and rained kisses from his neck to his shoulders, down further to his chest and the light dusting of hair leading to the bulge in his jeans. She knelt in front of him and kissed the hard bulge through his jeans.

He pulled her back up. "Not so fast."

He kissed her again, pulling her flush against him, his hands sliding to her bottom and squeezing gently. She moaned in the back of her throat, still a little sore from falling today but also loving the feel of his warm hands. He kept kissing her as he maneuvered her toward the bed. The back of her knees bumped the mattress. He broke the kiss and gave her a small shove so she landed on her back. She went up on her elbows, intending to slide up further on the mattress when his large hands on her hips stopped her.

"Lie back," he said in a husky voice.

She immediately dropped back and reached for him. "C'mere," she purred. "Get those jeans off."

"You're getting off first," he said, spreading her legs open to him.

"Jare—" Her breath caught as he knelt down, pulled her to the edge of the bed, and set her legs over his shoulders. "Oh!" His hot mouth took her in one intimate kiss, and then he set about making her crazed. His lips and tongue brought her to the edge again and again. She bucked wildly as he pushed her hard and then slowed things down again, pulling her back from the edge with a soft touch, the release she needed just out of reach.

"Don't stop!" she gasped.

He lifted his head, gazed into her eyes, and licked his lips. "You taste so good."

"I'm so close."

He grinned. "I know." He turned and kissed her inner thigh. "Maybe three times you were so close."

"Yes!" She gripped his hair and pulled him back where she wanted him. He nuzzled in, and she let out a long moan. The slow climb started again as his mouth worked its magic. She lifted her hips, open and needy. He obliged, amplifying the pleasure as he slid a finger inside her. "Yes!" she shouted as everything in her coiled and tightened. He pulled away.

She went up on her elbows and glared at him. "I'm going to scream if you don't—"

He tapped her hard nub with one finger, making her gasp. "You'll thank me when I finally give it to you."

"Please," she begged, lifting her hips. She'd never begged a man to take her before, but he made her feel desperate.

He ran his finger lazily up and down her sex, tracing the edges of where she needed him. "Please what?"

"Please give it to me."

"Give you…" He dropped a kiss just an inch higher than she needed. "What exactly?"

"Make me come!" She fisted her hand in his hair and pushed him down. He sucked gently, and arcs of electric sensation radiated out from the center of her world, traveling down her legs to her toes. She loosened her hold on him and threw her arms to her sides. He kept going, the gentle waves of pleasure radiating through her, making her moan softly as she floated in a haze of sensation. And then he slid his fingers inside of her, stroking her gently on the inside as he lapped at her. She tensed as she climbed that peak again, half afraid he'd stop, but he intensified his efforts, his fingers thrusting as his mouth closed firmly over her, and she exploded with a harsh cry as he kept going, letting her ride every last wave of pleasure until she had nothing left.

She was vaguely aware of him shifting her legs off his shoulders.

"You ready to thank me yet?" he asked, sounding entirely too boastful.

She half moaned, half laughed. "No."

"No?" he echoed. She heard the rasp of his zipper, and then his jeans hit the floor.

"You left me hanging too much." She sucked in a sharp breath as he cupped her firmly between the legs with one large hand.

"I guess you need someone to teach you some manners."

She couldn't speak. She was hot again, already revving up just at his firm hold.

He released her. "I'm really gonna have to work hard on you, aren't I?"

"No, you did plenty." She sat back on her elbows and took in his full naked glory for the first time as he stood at the end of the bed. He was magnificent, all sculpted muscle and golden skin from his wide shoulders and beautiful chest to his narrow waist, thick, muscled legs, and a massive erection. She quickly changed her mind. "Yes. Work hard on me."

She scrambled off the bed, wanting to touch him too. He pulled her flush against all that delicious naked glory and kissed her hard, his hands running all over her. She pulled back enough to grip his thick erection in one hand and felt him grow thicker. He lifted his head. "Em, wait."

She ignored him, giving him a nice stroking. "Maybe you'll thank me."

"Fuck, *wait*. I want you too much."

She stroked him again. He gripped her wrist, stilling her hand. "Condom," he ground out.

"I came prepared!" she announced, rushing to her suitcase and producing a box of them. She ripped it open and tossed him one before heading back toward the bed.

"C'mere," he said as he rolled it on. He was still standing next to the bed.

She changed direction, heading toward him, not sure what he had in mind and not caring. She wanted everything with him.

He grabbed the wood chair from the desk, set it in the center of the room, and sat down. He crooked a finger at her.

She stood in front of him. "Now what?"

He flashed a smile. "Ready for anything. I like it. See, this is why I had to make you grateful for your orgasm."

"Grateful!"

He grabbed her by the hips and brought her close, her breasts level with his face. "I'm gonna make you so grateful you'll be thanking me all night."

The laugh died in her throat as he suddenly captured her breast with his mouth, suckling hard enough to draw loud moans from her as she throbbed again. His other hand cupped her other breast and then clamped her nipple in a tight hold between his finger and thumb. She cried out at the sharp jolt of pleasure. He released his hold and moved his mouth to the other breast, suckling gently as his fingers slipped between her legs and stroked her over and over. She rocked into his hand. "Jared, take me. Please."

He lifted his head and gave her a slow, sexy smile. "I'm liking the please. All right, but I also want a thank you."

She ignored that, her aching need for him overriding everything else. She maneuvered herself up onto his lap, and he lifted her by the hips and positioned himself at her entrance, slowly easing her down. His size stretched her, filling her so completely and easing the ache she'd had for so long that she felt gratitude with every cell of her body. She wrapped her arms around his neck, gazed into his green eyes, and gave him a heartfelt, "Thank you."

He kissed her and nipped her bottom lip. "Thank *you*, darling." He moved her then, slowly riding her up and down his length, sending ripples of pleasure through her. She ran her hands up and down his arms, loving the flex and feel of his muscles under her hands as he continued to move her in slow, deep thrusts that only made her want more and more. Her breath caught as an orgasm snuck up on her. He stilled her before she hit the peak, grinding her down hard onto him, her body clasping him in a tight hold.

She smacked his shoulder frantically. "Please, thank you, please."

He chuckled before sinking his teeth into the cord of her neck. That set her off. She jerked her hips, and he loosened his hold, letting her ride him hard as she raced toward her release. His hands cupped her ass as he urged her on with the filthiest words she'd ever heard, making her feverish as her world narrowed down to that deep voice and the release that was frustratingly out of reach. "Jare," she said desperately.

He thrust up suddenly, giving her just the angle she needed, making her cry out as she broke hard, her body racked with pleasure for one endless wave before she collapsed against him. But he wasn't done. His hands went to her hips as he took over, making her take more as he thrust for his own release. She moaned and lifted her head as after-shocks shook her with unbearably intense waves of pleasure bringing another peak just as he shuddered and let go with a guttural groan, holding her tight against him.

She tried to catch her breath as she listened to his heart thundering in his chest.

After a few moments, he loosened his hold on her and kissed her hair. "I don't think once is going to be enough," he said in a hoarse voice.

"Definitely need more," she rasped out.

He gave her a tight hug. "Thank you."

Jared pulled on his boxer briefs and grabbed the hotel phone, ordering them room service dinner, trying to act like what just happened was no big deal. That was what Emily expected from him. A onetime fun time. She deserved a little fun in her life, and he was happy to be the one to give it to her.

Only his heart was in it now, raw and exposed.

She put on a white robe from the hotel, positively glow-ing. "Order champagne too!" She beamed. "I feel like cele-brating."

He added that to the order and hung up. He dressed

quickly, figuring he'd be the one to answer the door for room service. Besides, he liked having her in just the robe.

She crossed to him and threw her arms around his neck. "Why so serious? I thought you were Mr. Fun Time."

"Dr. Fun Time."

She ran her fingers through the hair at the nape of his neck. "I had fun. Did you?"

He forced a smile. "I did."

She whirled away and did a slow turn, her hands up to the sky in a joyful dance. He told himself to push down the swirl of deep emotions. That wasn't where she was at.

"You need some music," he said and turned on the radio alarm clock on the nightstand. It was already set to a top-forty pop station.

She laughed. "I love this song!" She danced all around, working her shoulders and hips in a sexy way that drew him in. He snagged her around the waist and pulled her close for a bit of grinding. She lifted her arms over her head as she moved in a sensuous wave in front of him. He moved in time with her.

"Ooh, baby!" she exclaimed.

He found himself smiling. "You like that?"

"I love it!"

He wedged his leg between hers and palmed her ass, letting her grind away. Her cheeks flushed, but she got into it.

"You're a great dancer," she told him when the song ended.

"That was all you." He pretty much stuck to slow dances, but grinding, that just came naturally. Another fast-paced song came on, and she grabbed his hand and twirled herself under it.

"You know," she said, releasing his hand to undulate right up against his front, making him rock hard, "we have the room all weekend so-o-oo—"

"So you want me to be Dr. Two-and-Done."

She grinned cheekily. "Or four." She danced in a circle around him.

"You're gonna kill me."

She reached his front and threw her arms around his neck. "You're so funny. Is this how you are with all the nurses? You make everyone grateful for the orgasm so it's *totally* worth it."

This seemed like a trick question. Women never liked to hear about other women. And, yes, that was exactly what he did. Held back until the orgasm hit with explosive force. Every single woman left his bedroom with a big smile. Except this woman he didn't want to let go.

He turned the question around. "Was it worth it?"

"Yes!" She gave him a smacking kiss on the lips. "Do that leg thing again." She started grinding against him. He thrust his leg between hers, giving her the friction she needed. Her eyes closed as a small smile played over her lips.

"Is this how you were with Angel?" He regretted the words the minute they were out of his mouth.

Her eyes flew open and she stilled. "What?"

He stepped back and shoved both hands in his hair. "Never mind."

She put her hands on her hips. "No, let's talk about this. Obviously it still bothers you that we were together. You want to know how it was with Angel? It was great. He's playful and fun and a dirty talker."

He did *not* want to know that. He pinched the bridge of his nose and closed his eyes. "I'm sorry. I shouldn't have brought it up."

"You want to know how my ex was too?"

He dropped his hand. "No!"

"He was selfish and always got off before I even got close. Happy? Now you know how you compare, so tell me how I measure up."

"Em—"

"Tell me!"

"No one can compare!" he barked.

They glared at each other. He wasn't sure who moved first, but one minute they were glaring and the next they slammed together, mouths fusing as they grabbed at each other's clothes, ripping them off before landing on the bed in a naked tangle of arms and legs. He rolled on top of her and took her in one hard thrust. She gasped, but he couldn't slow things down, just drove into her tight heat over and over, her moans and gasps making him wild. She clamped down on him suddenly and cried out as she went over the edge, taking him with her as he exploded, pumping into her on a long, low moan.

He stilled for a moment, buried deep inside her, wishing he could stay like that all night. Finally he raised his head to check in with her. He was never that rough, never lost control like that. "You okay?"

She smiled, eyes closed. "Oh yeah. I don't even care about dinner. I just want you, you, you all night long."

He kissed her, and she threw her arms around his neck and kissed him back with wild abandon.

His heart swelled with something that took his breath away. Or maybe that was her wild kisses. Either way he was down for the count. A complete goner.

## 10

Emily couldn't get enough of Jared. He definitely deserved the praise everyone threw on him. No wonder women lined up to be with him. She'd never wanted someone as much as she wanted him. Like an insatiable urge that drew her to him again and again. She'd climbed into his lap for their room service dinner, not wanting to stop touching him for even one minute. They were at the desk with their dinner, and Jared kept feeding her bites of his dinner and giving her sips of champagne. She felt positively giddy and was so glad she'd given herself this weekend of fun.

She ran her fingers through his soft hair. "I'm on the pill, so you don't have to worry about before."

He froze. "Shit. I didn't…I never…"

She kissed him. "It's okay."

He met her eyes. "I am so sorry. I got carried away. I didn't even think about it until just now. I always use protection. Always."

She smiled. "Good. Me too." She kissed his neck and tasted him, a little salty, a little sweet. "You taste so good."

"So do you…so, uh…"

She sucked his neck.

"Ah, Em."

She raised her head and smiled. "I'm riding bareback this weekend."

He groaned and claimed her mouth in a fierce possession. And then he stood with her in his arms and carried her to the bed, dinner forgotten.

Jared had never regretted the morning after as much as he did today. Emily was naked and curled up against his side. She was a spitfire once she got going. So enthusiastic, so eager to please, and all over him in the middle of the night and early this morning. He actually had to roll on top of her a few times to make any headway with what he wanted to do to her. He loved that she was so into it. And now it was over.

He didn't kid himself that they were on the same page here. She kept telling him how much fun he was and how this weekend was exactly what she needed for a fun break from her usual routine. He wasn't sure she'd even want to know his heart was involved. It seemed she was really happy with the Dr. One-and-Done experience. His rep was really biting him in the ass this time.

She stirred and rubbed a hand over his chest. "Mmm...." She opened her soft brown eyes and gave him a lazy, sexy smile. "Ready for more?" She slid her hand to his cock, which was ready from the minute he woke up next to her naked body.

He pushed her hand away. "My heart can't take it," he said in bald-faced honesty. Then he rolled out of bed and headed for the shower.

He'd just stepped into the steamy spray when Emily appeared, naked and smiling, and then stepped in with him. Fucked. He was fucked. She wrapped her arms around his neck and pressed herself against him. One more time, he told himself as he claimed her mouth. Just once more. Her hot little mouth trailed to his throat, which she nipped and licked. He pinned her against the shower wall and became the aggressor. She groaned and mewled, setting him on fire. He couldn't wait. Just lifted her and took her right there. He lost himself. There was nothing but this miraculous joining that made him feel he was finally, finally home. When they finished, panting and clinging to each other, all he could think was somehow he had to tell her he wanted more with her. But he was at a loss for the right words.

"Can you put me down?" she asked, still breathing hard. "I'm starting to lose feeling in my legs."

He set her back on her feet. Her knees buckled, but he caught her and held her steady.

She let out a shaky laugh. "See what you do to me?" Her brown eyes were bright and happy.

"Em." He cleared his throat. "Emily…" He trailed off, unsure how to say he didn't want to be the good-time guy with her.

But then she started washing him with her cat-that-ate-the-canary look, and he got distracted. And, of course, he had to return the delicious scrubbing, and then they started kissing and didn't stop until the water started to run cold.

"We should get dry," she said.

He followed her out and grabbed a towel. She was already wrapped up in a towel, and he missed the view.

"Oh!" she exclaimed. "That's my cell."

He hadn't even heard the ring. All he could focus on was her.

She ran to the bedroom and was quiet for a long time. He stepped out of the bathroom, drying his hair. She was dressing in a frantic rush.

"What's wrong?" he asked.

"Chris is in PICU. He took a turn for the worse." Shit. That was the pediatric intensive care. She looked around frantically. "Where are my shoes?" she cried.

"Calm down." He fetched her shoes from the corner where she'd left them.

"We have to go. Like right now."

"Got it." He dressed quickly, grabbed their stuff scattered around the room, and headed out.

"I never should've taken off this weekend," she said as

they pulled out of the parking lot. "This never would've happened on my watch. I just had to have a fun weekend. Now look what happened."

"It's not your fault."

"I have a serious job. That means a serious life. Not frivolous ski weekends. Not hookups with players."

"I won't...Em—"

"He can't die. Faster, Jared!"

He pushed the speed limit. Some part of him knew if Emily lost her patient, she'd cut him loose for good. Her heart wasn't in it, not like his was.

Jared dropped Emily off at the hospital and went home absolutely miserable. Emily fiercely regretted their weekend away. Told him she'd been foolish and they could never happen again. He didn't know what to do.

He dragged his sorry ass to Sunday dinner and went through the motions, barely hearing the conversation that flowed around him. Something about Kennedy's new rockstar client everyone was curious about.

He finished his dinner in silence and was about to make an excuse to leave during a brief lull in the conversation when his mom asked, "Jared, Angel, how was your ski weekend?"

*Awesome. Soul crushing.* He didn't know how to answer.

Angel answered for him. "I didn't go. Jared went with Emily."

Jared shot Angel a look across the table that said *thanks a lot*.

Angel mouthed, *what?*

"Emily, the woman who was here for dinner?" his mom asked, her voice rising on a high note of excitement.

Jared kept his mouth shut. He didn't want to talk about Emily in front of his brothers, who would tease him mercilessly. He'd give them the same treatment. In fact, he had on plenty of occasions.

"The one you two fought over?" Luke asked with a smirk.

"Interesting. So…don't keep us in suspense, did you close the deal?"

"Shut up," Jared snapped.

"He didn't," Nico said. Luke nodded.

"Now we don't know that for sure," Vince said. "Maybe he's being discreet."

His brothers laughed uproariously.

Their mom cleared her throat loudly. "Gentlemen, this conversation is unseemly, especially in front of other women." She gestured to their sisters-in-law, who were all trying to look properly offended. "Jared, would you like to invite her for dinner? We could make it on a Friday or Saturday so it's intimate. I could bake—"

"No!" Jared barked. His mom liked to bake Italian wedding cookies that, so far, had caused three marriages after his brothers and their girlfriends ate them. It was kinda spooky. His brothers all exchanged conspiratorial looks and grinned.

"Watch that tone," his stepdad, Vinny, said. His family was big on respect and manners.

"Sorry, Mom," Jared said. "I meant no, thank you." He caught Angel's sympathetic eyes and felt a little better. At least Angel wouldn't razz him about Emily.

"So the weekend didn't go well?" Angel asked casually.

Jared ground his teeth. "It went fine."

"If it was fine, then why the long face?" Vince asked.

Jared glanced around the table at his entire family looking at him with a mixture of barely disguised amusement (his brothers minus Angel) and sympathy (his mom, sisters-in-law, and Angel).

"Did you tease her too much?" Luke asked. "You do step over the line a lot." He turned to his fiancée, Kennedy. "Didn't I say he needed sensitivity training?"

Kennedy nodded and turned to Jared. "Did she say she didn't want to see you again?"

"I dunno." He peeled the label off his beer and crumpled it in his hand.

"What does that mean, I don't know?" Kennedy asked. "Why don't you know? Did you ask her for another date?"

Jared sent Luke a significant look. Luke raised his palms like he was helpless to control his woman. Everyone was still staring at him, so Jared blurted, "She feels guilty for going away for the weekend because her patient ended up in PICU. That's the pediatric intensive care."

Angel froze, beer bottle halfway to his mouth. "Oh. I'm sorry to hear that. That's terrible."

Jared stared at the table. "Yeah."

"She's probably just upset," Angel said. "Give her a little time."

Everyone agreed with that assessment, which wasn't at all helpful. Because the real problem, he'd realized, was him. Emily knew his rep and didn't want to get burned after her ex. He was fun for a weekend. That was it.

Jared stood with his dishes. "I'm going to go. Thanks for dinner."

He headed to the kitchen. Angel appeared at his side as he was loading the dishes in the dishwasher. "You guys just need to talk things out."

Jared bit back a sarcastic reply to Mr. Feelings Talker. He knew Angel was just trying to help. He straightened. "Thanks, but it's not that simple."

"Reassure her you won't cheat," Angel said. "That's a hot-button issue for her."

Jared huffed. "As much as I *love* talking things out with you about the woman we both screwed, I'm leaving." Never mind that he'd had the brilliant idea to get advice from Angel before. Now everything sucked. He headed toward the front door.

"Give her more fun times," Angel called. "Wear her down."

*Fun times.* Jared scowled, especially irritated because Emily had said Angel was fun in bed. He turned. "She doesn't want that. She just wants to go back to her life."

"Geez, you can't give up. Just make it happen."

Jared turned and pulled open the front door. If it were that easy, he wouldn't feel like hell right now.

"I'll talk to her," Angel said.

Jared slammed the door and did an about-face. "Don't you dare. That's…" He trailed off. *Awkward and inappropriate from her former ideal lover.* Geez, this was so twisted. "I'll deal with it."

Angel crossed to him and lowered his voice. "I feel responsible. I pushed you toward her. I really thought she'd be good for you."

"She was," he said over the lump in his throat.

"And I thought you'd be good for her."

He swallowed hard. "I'm not."

Angel looked thoughtful. "Give it some time. I know there's something there."

"You don't know that! You never even saw us together."

"Yes, I did, at Sunday dinner and at cooking class. She lights up when you're around. And you get the soft eyes." He jabbed a finger at him. "I'll fix this, Jare. Don't give up hope."

"Don't do anything! I don't want any surprises, no showing up at Sunday dinner, and for God's sake, don't even think about bringing Mom and her voodoo cookies into this."

Angel smiled widely. "Now there's an idea."

"No! You wouldn't want me to push your thing with Julia."

Angel's brown eyes flashed. "Don't go there!"

"I will if you don't drop it!"

"Are they fighting again?" Vince boomed, appearing in the hallway. There was a sudden murmur of male voices.

"No betting!" his mom exclaimed.

Angel's whole expression dimmed. He turned away.

Jared instantly felt remorse. "Ah, Ang, I'm sorry. I shouldn't have—"

Angel went back to rejoin their family and flipped him the bird over his shoulder. Vince shook his head at Jared.

Jared left, feeling like a major screwup. First with Emily and now with Angel.

# 11

Emily was absolutely haunted by Chris. Not only because she couldn't stop thinking about his frail little body sitting in PICU while she was off having the time of her life, but also because it hit a little too close to home from when her patient Jaden died two years ago. Jaden had also ended up in PICU when she was away. He'd died three days later.

She'd visited Chris as soon as she got back. Not surprisingly, Chris's dad, Tony, held vigil at Chris's side. Chris was the center of his dad's world. He was an only child, and his mom had died in childbirth having him.

"Hi, Tony," she said gently.

He looked up, his brown hair greasy, his eyes bloodshot with dark rings of fatigue under them. "Emily," he said, his voice rough and gravelly like he hadn't spoken in a while, "you came."

"Of course I did. I'll check in on him daily."

"You will? What time?"

"Whenever I can get my break."

"Here, take my seat. He'll want to hear from you."

Tony changed places with her, standing at the foot of Chris's bed while she took the chair next to the bed. Chris was sleeping, his small body frail and fragile. She held his bony hand and spoke to him anyway. "Hey, buddy. It's Emily.

You can relax. We're taking good care of you. Your dad is here to be sure of it." She heard a choking sob and saw Tony had broken down in tears, one hand clapped over his mouth. She knew it was hell to watch his only child suffering. She turned back to Chris. "The Christmas lights are up around town. We're going to put some in your room too, all white and twinkling like stars. Or snowflakes. You know, each snowflake is unique and special. Like you." She swallowed over the awful lump in her throat. "Olivia made you a friendship bracelet and—"

"He won't be alone if he goes," Tony said in a hoarse voice.

She nodded, glancing at Tony's red tear-streaked face before turning back to Chris. She knew what he meant. Tony had said before that Chris's mother would be waiting for him in heaven. "That's right, Chris. All the people who love you will always be there for you." Her throat choked up too much to speak any further. She gave Chris's hand a small squeeze and stood.

She gestured for Tony to take her spot.

"Don't go," he said. "I don't want to be alone right now, and Chris has always loved you."

"Okay." How could she say no? She stayed a while longer until she was paged to go back to work. "I'm sorry, I really have to go. I'll be back."

Tony nodded gravely and resumed his vigil in the chair next to his son. "We'll be here."

It had been a week, and Chris was hanging on, but he was drifting in and out of consciousness.

Jared had texted her a few times and even tried to have lunch with her in the hospital cafeteria, but she shut him down. She just couldn't deal with it all. It wasn't that she didn't feel something for him. If she was honest with herself, she'd felt too much. In opening herself to a fun weekend with him, she'd inadvertently opened her heart and got slammed for it with the news about Chris. Clearly she was not meant for that kind of carefree life. And Chris had paid for her selfishness.

She didn't kid herself she was some kind of miracle worker, but she monitored her patients closely and was quick to respond to any change, for better or worse. Many times that quick response had made a difference. She'd gone over Chris's chart, and while the hospital wasn't at fault for being negligent, they hadn't responded quickly or aggressively enough, in her opinion. Not like she would have advocated for if she'd been there.

She drooped home Friday night only to find her ex-husband, Michael, waiting on her doorstep. There were no reporters, no cameras, just him standing there holding a gold box wrapped with a blue ribbon. He wore a gray wool coat over his suit. Too exhausted to rail against him, too frazzled for a confrontation, she merely stared at the gold box. As she got closer, she saw it was Godiva. Her favorite chocolate. He'd finally gotten it right.

"Hi, Emily," he said when she reached his side. "These are for you."

She took the box and broke down in tears.

"What is it?" Michael asked, guiding her to the stairs to sit down. "Are these happy or sad tears?"

That just made her cry harder. Three years of marriage, and he still had no clue whether she was happy or sad.

He put an arm around her. "Did I get the wrong kind of chocolate? My assistant said…"

She covered her face with her hands and sobbed. But she wasn't crying over him. Not really. It was just the push she needed to get out her grief over Chris.

"What can I do?" he asked.

She kept right on crying. Not up to explaining anything.

"Okay," he said and just sat with her, one arm wrapped around her.

She cried until she had no more tears and then leaned against his side, exhausted.

"Want to talk about it?" he asked.

She sniffled. "One of my patients…he…I'm not sure he's going to make it."

"Didn't I tell you to get a thicker skin for your job?"

She clenched her jaw. He'd always said she was too sensitive. But she was only good at her job because she felt so much for her patients. He'd never understand that because the man had no emotions.

She straightened. "Why are you here?"

"I wanted to see you."

"Why?"

"My therapist says you might need an apology before you'll consider a reconciliation."

"Seriously?"

"I'm sorry if I've caused you any pain from my actions."

"You betrayed me, Michael."

"I know. I'm sorry."

"You humiliated me in the press."

"That wasn't my intention. The press went a little nuts. I have no control over that."

She stood.

"Wait!" He stood too. "I've changed. I can be satisfied without going outside our relationship. With whatever you're comfortable with."

*Yeah, right.* "Thanks for the chocolate."

"If you were married to me, you wouldn't have to work that cancer job anymore. That job is going to kill you."

"Supportive as ever," she said before striding to her door. She stopped and looked back to where Michael was still standing watching her. "I met someone. Don't come here again."

And with that she went into her apartment. Not that she thought anything more would happen with Jared. She was a hot mess. Her life was a hot mess. The last thing she needed was another complication. She just wanted to get Michael off her back.

She waited a few minutes to see if he'd follow or knock on the door, but he must've left. She breathed a sigh of relief and dove into the chocolate. Then she poured a glass of wine to take the edge off. She conked out on the sofa a short while later in a massive sugar crash.

She woke to the sound of her cell phone ringing the next

morning. She snatched it up and saw not only had she over-slept for her Saturday shift, but she had numerous voicemails and texts from her friends Charlotte and Megan.

*Is this photoshopped?* Charlotte asked in a text next to an image of what appeared to be her and Michael cozying up to each other. Someone must've gotten a picture of when she was leaning against his side with his arm around her last night. You couldn't tell that she was crying. The angle of her face and body just looked like she was leaning into his embrace. Shit.

She texted back her friends and then rushed to the shower to get ready. She couldn't deal with this right now. Her patients needed her. Obviously Michael was still spinning stories in the press about them. She was sure they'd be all over a possible reconciliation. The scandal was too juicy to bypass any speculation about them. Now she'd have to issue another statement. Maybe she should look into that restraining order. He hadn't hurt her, but he was definitely harassing her. She wasn't sure how to go about doing that. Augh. She had the worst headache from overindulging and stress.

She popped a couple of ibuprofen, washed them down with orange juice, and grabbed a granola bar to eat on the way to work. She had to put Michael out of her mind and focus on what was important. Kids depended on her.

When she got to work, she snagged the goody bag for Jared's visit and steeled herself against any of his charming smiles. She was in no mood for that crazy roller coaster. No matter how exhilarating the ride, she couldn't handle the inevitable fall.

Jared showed up for his Captain Huddle visit on Saturday with a tangle of emotions messing with his head. He had to be there for the kids and knew how important his visit was now that one of their friends had ended up in PICU. At the same time, he was beside himself with the news story he'd seen this morning with a picture of Emily cozied up to her ex.

Seriously, of all the people for her to be with! Just thinking about it pissed him off especially because she'd told Jared she had to dedicate all of her time to her patients. He'd done nothing but show her a good time. Her ex had cheated on her and humiliated her. Clearly the woman wasn't in her right mind because of her grief over Chris. They were going to talk things out, as Angel had told him to in the first place. He should've listened to Mr. Feelings Talker. He wasn't sure exactly what he'd say to Emily, but he was sure something would come to him. Failure was not an option.

He spotted her by the nurses' station, waiting for him with the goody bag. He closed the distance between them quickly and kissed her cheek. "Hey, Em."

"Ooh!" a young girl voice squealed.

Emily stiffened. Jared turned to see ten-year-old Olivia walking with an IV. A young blond nurse walked with her. "Captain Huddle kissed Emily!" Olivia exclaimed.

"Don't do that again," Emily hissed under her breath to Jared before saying to Olivia, "That's because I gave him extra-special prizes for well-behaved children."

"Captain Huddle and Emily sitting in a tree," Olivia sang.

Jared chuckled. He liked the direction this song was heading.

"Happy now?" Emily asked him. "Now I'll never hear the end of it."

"K-I-S-S-I-N-G," Olivia sang loudly before the nurse at her side quieted her.

"Meet me after your shift," he said. "We need to talk."

She rubbed her temple. "I'm really not up for this. You have no idea—"

"Em—"

"Please don't."

"First comes love," Olivia sang a little quieter.

Emily pointed a warning finger at Olivia then turned to Jared and said quietly, "Just treat me like one of your nurses. Okay? I can't handle more than that right now."

"I would if I could. Believe me, it would be easier." He leaned close and didn't miss the pink flush that rose in her cheeks. "You think I wanted this to happen?" He was halfway in love with the woman, their chemistry was off the charts, and she was cozied up to her ex.

She huffed. "I'm sorry Angel forced me on you."

He shook his head. "I didn't mean it like that."

Emily's lips twitched, and she reached up and patted his quilled hat. Damn. He kept forgetting he was in costume around her.

"Then comes marriage," Olivia sang over her shoulder before disappearing around the corner.

"After your shift," he said, pushing up his eye mask to meet her eyes directly, "I'm coming for you."

She shivered. *Good.* At least she knew he was serious about talking stuff out. He slammed the eye mask down and whirled, cape flying behind him as he headed for the first room. He sent a silent prayer up to PICU for Chris. This would be the first time he hadn't visited Chris's room. He swallowed hard and strode into little Candace's room.

"Anyone here like butterflies?" he asked in a cheerful voice.

Emily would not be meeting up with Jared after her shift. He was too tempting, even in a ridiculous porcupine costume. She went back to work, pushing him out of her mind, but an hour later she ran into him in the hallway.

He leaned down to her ear, his voice a sexy rumble. "Meet me in the break room after your shift."

"No."

"Fine, I'll meet you, and then we'll go to my place and talk."

She kept her voice low. "I have no intention of going to your place to quote, unquote talk."

His scowl was made less intimidating by the fact that he was dressed like a porcupine. "We're talking."

She put up a hand in the universal *stop* sign and went back to work. Her patients needed her complete focus, and that was exactly what they'd get.

When her shift ended, she walked quickly past the break room, not daring to see if Jared was in there waiting for her, and speedwalked to the elevator, heart pounding. He could be very persistent.

The doors opened to an empty elevator, and she dashed inside, punching the button for the main floor. She took a deep breath and told herself to calm down. Like a sixth sense she met his green eyes as he strode toward her, not wearing the absurd costume, just a blue long-sleeved shirt that emphasized his broad shoulders with worn jeans. He carried a duffel bag crammed full, and the determined look in his eyes said *I've got you now.* She frantically punched the button for the main floor. *Come on, come on.*

The doors began to close, and then a large sneakered foot wedged between them and they opened.

"Hello, Emily," he said in a dangerously soft voice.

"Hi," she squeaked.

As soon as the doors shut, he dropped the bag and advanced on her, backing her up against the wall and boxing her in with his hands on either side of her hips. She heated everywhere. It was like she couldn't control her response to him.

His mouth grazed her ear as he asked, "What's a guy gotta do to get some words with you?"

"There's nothing we need to talk about," she said, her voice coming out embarrassingly breathy. *Get a hold of yourself. You don't have time for this.*

His green eyes met hers in one intense look. "I saw you with your ex."

"That's over."

"You looked pretty cozy."

She stared at his mouth. Suddenly she wanted nothing more than to lose herself in his kisses.

"Are you with him?" Jared asked.

"No."

His large hand cradled her cheek. "Good. You deserve better."

"Like you?"

"Like me." He kissed her cheek, his fingers sliding into her hair, holding her in place.

Her eyelids fluttered down. "I don't want to talk…" She swallowed, finding it difficult to think. She was supposed to focus on her patients. Jared was too distracting. "I need to focus on work right now."

"Work's over for today," he said before slamming his mouth over hers.

His mouth took possession, his tongue sweeping inside. She caved and threw her arms around his neck, kissing him back like he was the last life vest in the despairing hellhole of her life.

The doors opened with a *ding*.

Jared grabbed his bag and took her hand, guiding her out the door and toward the hospital exit. Her knees felt like jelly. She was throbbing and desperately needed more.

"My place?" he asked when they stepped outside into the cold December air.

She hesitated as her brain struggled to kick in. She was going to regret this, right?

He cupped the back of her neck, leaned down and whispered in her ear, "I'll teach you some manners."

She ached, remembering how he made her beg *please* and then thank him for a monster orgasm. The throbbing intensified. She could really use the stress relief.

She met his eyes. "Yes, please."

He chuckled and grabbed her hand, leading her toward his house.

Jared was torn between finding out more about Emily and her ex, which would probably piss him off, and shutting his damn mouth because it looked like he was going to get Emily in his bed again very soon. The heat between them was insane. But then before they'd even reached his house, he blurted out, "So tell me exactly why your ex-husband had his arm around you."

"This again?"

"Yes."

"He came over—"

"He came over!" He stopped dead in his tracks. He hadn't realized the picture was taken at her apartment. "Did you *invite* him over?"

"No."

"So he just showed up?"

"Yes."

"And then what?"

"He gave me chocolate, and I cried. He was comforting me. And he apologized."

His hands were in fists, and he forced himself to loosen up. "Em, be straight with me. Is this thing with you and your ex still going on?"

"Nope, no way, no how."

He studied her for a moment, and she gazed back at him unflinchingly. He believed her, but still. Obviously she didn't hate her ex if she let him comfort her. The fact that she'd pushed Jared away when he'd tried to do the same hurt more than he'd thought possible.

Jared swallowed hard. "There's a bunch of news stories saying you're on your way to a reconciliation."

"Are you going to believe me or the press?" she snapped.

"You, but—" He stopped himself. "I don't want you to see him anymore," he bit out.

"That's pretty high-handed of you. Just laying down the law after we slept together one time."

"Five times."

She threw her hands up. "Whatever!"

"You call me if he shows up again. I'll make him listen."

"Jared, no," she said in a choked voice. She swiped at her eyes. "Now I'm getting upset again. I thought you were going to help me forget—"

He kissed her, immediately realizing his mistake, and she

kissed him back passionately. Emily needed him to be the fun hookup guy. So that was exactly what he'd be. They'd talk later, once she was more relaxed, though he didn't tell her that. She wrapped her arms around his neck and leaned her whole body against him, so he knew he'd made her feel better. He broke the kiss, took her hand, and led her to his place.

No sooner had he shut the door behind her than she launched herself at him. He caught her, turned and pressed her against the door.

Their mouths fused together and things got crazy. Her hands were all over him as he ripped off her pants and panties. He was inside her within minutes, not even completely undressed as he pounded against her while she moaned and gasped and urged him on.

She went off fast, and he just let go, taking what he needed until he was spent. Only Emily made him lose control like that. He rested his forehead against hers, and she smiled.

"Thank you," she said. "I needed the stress relief."

He cupped her jaw with one hand. "Is that all I am to you?" He didn't mean to get so serious so fast, but there it was. He couldn't *just* be the fun time for her. No matter how much more convenient that would be. For both of them.

She closed her eyes and tipped her head back.

He pulled out and set her back on her feet, keeping his hands on her arms in case her knees buckled. "Answer me."

She searched his face, and he stared back at her with all the deep feelings he had. "I'm sorry," she said. "I just relaxed for the first time all week. I didn't mean anything by it."

She pulled away and headed for the sofa, where he'd tossed her scrub pants and panties. "So I guess I'll be going."

"Stay."

She pulled on her panties. "Why?"

He struggled for the right words. *Because I feel stuff. Like with Jen before she dumped me. No, she doesn't want to hear about your ex.*

"For the stress relief," he blurted.

She smiled. "I feel fine now." She reached for her pants,

and he moved quickly to stop her. He tossed them to the side, gripped her by the hair and kissed her hard. She melted against him. He kept going, thrusting his leg between hers, intent on one thing only, sealing her to him. She was still revved from earlier and was soon moaning and rocking her hips rhythmically against his leg. He kept kissing her as she mewled in the back of her throat, and the moment he felt her tense on the edge of her peak, he pulled away.

She grabbed for him frantically, off balance, and he held her upright.

"So you'll stay," he said. They'd talk later. Much later.

She nodded, her cheeks flushed.

"Come on, I'll feed you lunch before I screw your brains out. I'll take you on the counter next time."

"Y-yeah. That sounds good."

He chuckled. "Thought you might like that."

After two exhilarating Venus services with Jared, Emily had to go to the Christmas cooking class she'd signed up for at Ludbury House in Clover Park. She considered not going because Jared was such a nice distraction from all her worry over Chris. It was damn hard to feel good about anything when a child she cared about suffered. Chris had been through so much with chemo and painful bone-marrow treatments. But it really did help her cope better by focusing on something normal in her life, like cooking. To her surprise, Jared had also signed up for the class.

"Seriously?" she asked. "I didn't think you liked to cook. I've only seen you make ham and cheese sandwiches."

He wrapped his arms around her from behind, pushed her hair to the side, and kissed the side of her neck. "And what's wrong with ham and cheese sandwiches?"

"Nothing. I just…" She trailed off as he lifted her hair and kissed the nape of her neck, causing a frisson of sensation down her spine. "You have to stop touching me, or I'll never get to class."

He chuckled and moved to her ear, running his tongue along the shell. "That sounds like an invitation."

She turned in his arms. He gave her a small smile, his warm green eyes alight with mischief, dimples showing in his stubbled cheeks. "You're not just trying to keep me from Josh, are you?" She knew he hadn't liked the bartender flirting with her.

He scratched his head. "Who's Josh?" He didn't fool her for one minute.

"Yeah, okay. Let's go. I need to stop home for some fresh clothes."

After Jared parked the truck in her apartment complex's parking lot, she turned to him. "Wait here, I'll just be a minute."

She walked briskly up the stairs and stopped short at her front door. There was a brown teddy bear sitting on the welcome mat with a red stitched heart. This couldn't be from Jared, he'd been with her most of the day. She quickly looked around for signs of Michael, but she was alone. She scooped it up and noticed a folded note taped to the back. With shaking hands, she opened the small piece of paper that read in tiny all caps printed letters, *For Emily, a very special woman.*

She swallowed hard and dashed into her apartment. It didn't look like Michael's writing. Of course, he could've had his assistant write it, or maybe it was delivered and the person at the shop wrote it. She stashed the bear on the top shelf of the hall closet in case she needed it for evidence. *Calm down.* Maybe it was from Jared. He could've ordered it earlier. Or from Josh. Or…Michael had gone off the deep end.

She quickly threw on a red sweater with a black skirt, black pantyhose, and flats, hoping the cheery outfit would help her get into the holiday class. She told herself not to panic. It could be anyone that sent her a teddy bear. It didn't have to be anything bad. She tried to focus on the good: she was going to a festive cooking class. She suddenly felt woozy and sat down.

A short while later, she climbed back into the warm truck. Jared had switched the station to one playing Christmas carols, which gave her a warm and fuzzy feeling despite her worry over the teddy bear gift and Chris.

Jared glanced over at her. "Hey, you okay?" He was surprisingly in tune with her moods.

"Yeah." She didn't want to tell him about the teddy bear. It was probably nothing. And she really didn't need him going all caveman and going after Michael. She had no proof.

She stared out the window as Jared pulled onto the main road out of the apartment complex, still a little shaken up, and found herself asking, "Do you think I'm special?" *A very special woman.* She watched his expression, kind of hoping he'd suddenly grin and know she was talking about the gift, that it was from him after all and she could stop freaking out, but he just looked confused and a little uncomfortable.

He cleared his throat. "Uh, what do you mean special? Special how?"

"Never mind."

"Sure, you're special. Am I special?"

It wasn't him with the teddy bear message. He acted like he'd never thought about someone being special before. "Sure."

"Feel better now?"

"Not really." She blew out a breath. "I'm still worried about Chris."

"He's hanging on."

"So far."

The frustration and helplessness washed over her again, pulling her back to that dark, despairing place. Jared reached over and squeezed her hand.

A few minutes later, he broke into her whirl of worried and despairing thoughts. "Check out the lights."

Main Street in Clover Park was lit up with white lights wrapped around the old-fashioned street lamps and trees lining both sides of the street.

"It's beautiful," she said.

"They always do up Ludbury House too for the holidays," he said.

A few minutes later, they arrived at Ludbury House. The

white house was decorated with white lights, as were all the trees on the property, including a huge thirty-foot pine tree. The wrought-iron fence lining the front of the property held festive greenery with red velvet bows.

Jared took her hand as they walked inside, holding the heavy wooden door open for her. A large Christmas tree decorated with white lights and red bows filled the foyer. Brightly wrapped gifts with gold bows were piled under it. The grand staircase had greenery wrapped around the banister.

"Welcome back to Ludbury House!" Hailey greeted them joyfully. She wore a green velvet elf hat with fake elf ears sewn onto the sides of the hat and a matching green velvet dress. She handed elf hats to both of them.

Jared put his elf hat on. He looked ridiculously cute. It brought out the green in his eyes.

Hailey's blue eyes lit up as she looked from Jared to Emily. "Are you two together?"

Emily didn't know how to answer that.

Jared answered for her. "Yes." He took the elf hat out of Emily's clenched fist and settled it on her head. His eyes held hers in challenge of his claim. After the afternoon she'd spent gasping and panting with his hard body pressed against hers, it wasn't so easy to deny it.

Hailey clapped, breaking the spell. "Wonderful!" She handed Emily her card. "In case you need it."

She glanced down at a cream-colored business card embossed with silver bells that read *Hailey Adams*, and then under that, *Love Junkie*.

"I'm a wedding planner," Hailey explained. "Go on back to the kitchen."

Emily shoved the card in her purse, cheeks burning in mortification. She didn't want Jared to read something into that since she was never getting married again. She quickly changed the subject. "I wonder what we'll be learning to cook tonight."

"I hope it's dessert," Jared said. He took her hand,

entwining his fingers with hers, as he walked to the kitchen with her. "It feels like we're together, right?"

She did *not* want to get into a discussion about that right now. She still wasn't sure how she ended up hooking up with him a second time after regretting their little weekend fling. The only reasonable explanation was the extreme stress she was under, but she didn't think he'd like to hear he was her stress reliever. He'd seemed angry when she'd blurted that out before.

"Ho-ho-ho," Shane, their chef instructor, said, greeting them with a wave. He wore a Santa hat over his red hair. "You're back."

Emily waved to him and to his grandmother, Maggie, who wore an elf hat over her short white hair and a green velvet dress that matched Hailey's. "I'm the elf-off-the-shelf!" Maggie proclaimed. "Or is it off my rocker?" She slapped her knee, pleased with her joke.

Emily giggled. Maggie actually did resemble a happy elf with her petite size and cheerful demeanor. She caught sight of Julia quietly tying an apron on in the corner. "Hi, Julia."

"Hi," Julia said in a soft voice.

"Hey, Julia," Jared said. "Angel coming tonight?"

She nodded. "He'll be here."

The stainless steel prep table in the center of the room was covered with thin bars of chocolate, chocolate chips, sugar, flour, and tubes of icing. Looked like dessert to her. She looked to Jared, who grinned.

"We had two couples cancel on us, so it'll be a small group tonight," Shane said. "Some kind of flu going around. Grab an apron."

Jared grabbed an apron for himself and one for her, and they put them on.

Just then Josh, the bartender from Garner's, arrived wearing an elf hat. He looked strange in it; the cute hat paired with a flannel shirt over ripped jeans made him look like a badass biker with an elf fetish.

"I really hope we'll be baking cookies in a tree," Josh said with a grin.

"Keebler elves!" Maggie crowed.

Josh pointed at his nose like *ding, ding, ding, right answer!*

Julia giggled, which seemed to encourage Josh as he crossed to her. "Dangerous profession, isn't it?" He smiled down at Julia. "Where's your elf hat?"

She shook her head. "I took it off to put on the apron."

Josh looked over to the aprons, spotted her hat and retrieved it for her. Then he settled it on her head and smoothed her hair off her cheeks and over her ears. Julia flushed bright pink. "Adorable," Josh pronounced, which made the pink tinge with red.

"Nice hat," a voice barked from the doorway. Emily turned to see Angel in his black leather jacket, striding in like he wanted to kick someone's ass.

Jared whistled under his breath.

Julia quickly took off her hat.

Hailey followed on Angel's heels. "Your boyfriend's here, Julia!" she caroled.

Julia glanced at Josh and then to Angel. "We're just friends."

"Yes," Angel bit out. "Best friends."

"Oh." Hailey looked at Josh, who was smiling and looking at Julia, who was blushing furiously again. Hailey pressed a card into Julia's hand. "Call me. I can help you with that."

Angel looked pleased. So did Josh.

"Thank you," Julia said. She took one look at the card, made a tiny squeak, and then looked around the room at all the curious faces. "I'll just go put this in my purse." She dashed to the corner where she'd stashed her purse.

"All righty, then," Maggie announced. "Tonight is for desserts."

"Yes!" Jared said with a fist pump.

Maggie laughed. "We'll start with my world-famous fudge, a simple recipe, while Shane gets things ready for a traditional Yule log. A lot more work, but ultimately worth it."

"Quality cooking can't be rushed," Shane said.

"Nothing good can be rushed," Maggie said with a wink. "Am I right, ladies?"

Julia blushed.

Emily spoke up. "Slow is good."

Josh slid her a sultry look across the room, and then Jared's arm settled around her shoulders. Nothing like the caveman routine to get a woman going. Not that Jared had to do all that much to get her going. He spent the rest of the class touching her as they worked together on their desserts—a hand squeeze, a quick brush down her back, pushing her hair back over her shoulder, touching her arm. She had a feeling he had more in store for her tonight, even though she knew spending the night with him would be a bad idea. She had to give them some space before she got too attached. She knew his rep, after all. And spending another weekend with him would give him the wrong message. It was a fun, onetime thing. Okay, five times.

Plus two more. Whatever.

She forced her focus back to class. Several hours later, their Yule logs were complete. It was basically a thin chocolate cake rolled like a jelly roll, but instead of jelly, they made a sweet cream filling. They frosted the whole thing with milk chocolate icing, using the tines of the fork to make it resemble a log, and then decorated it with icing holly and berries. Hers and Jared's was a mess and lopsided, mostly because Jared kept fooling around, making it difficult to focus. Angel and Julia's turned out perfect. Josh had worked with Maggie, and theirs was also perfect, though it had way too much whipped cream swirled on top because Maggie was really into whipped cream. She kept hinting at all of its other uses, which made Josh laugh and the rest of them fidget uncomfortably at the idea of senior-citizen nooky.

Class finished, and Jared fetched her coat and helped her on with it. She was surprised at his gentlemanly manners until she realized with a heated flush that he was pretty big on manners. She wondered if he'd ask if she wanted to be driven home or go back to his place. After the way he kept touching her and smiling at her all through class, and the fact that she was still a little freaked out about her teddy bear gift, she was leaning toward his place.

Jared glanced over at Angel, who was glaring at Josh, who was openly flirting with a blushing Julia as they all got ready to leave cooking class.

"Give me a minute," he told Emily.

He was a little worried Angel would get into it with Josh. Angel had that murderous look he got just before he swung a fist. It took a lot to get his stepbrother to that level of rage, but once he was there, it was tough to pull him back.

He snagged Angel by the sleeve of his leather jacket and pulled him away. "Hey, how's it going?"

"What?" Angel snapped.

"How's it going? Things good?"

Angel blew out a breath. "I wasn't going to touch him."

Jared socked him on the arm. "Good."

Angel socked him back. Hard. "Yeah, good." His attention strayed back to Julia, who was saying something in a low voice to Josh and shaking her head. Angel started toward her, but Jared held him back, one hand on his shoulder. Angel shook him off and was about to stalk over there when Josh inclined his head at Julia with a smile, turned, and left.

"She handled it," Jared said in a low voice.

Angel nodded once. "Guy's a jerk."

"He's just being a guy. Can't blame him for trying." He could say that easily now that *he* was the one hooking up with Emily.

Angel scowled. "How's it going with Emily?"

He couldn't help but smile. "Great." He glanced over to where Emily was now chatting with Maggie. Emily was smiling and it made him happy to see her happy. He'd really been worried about the downturn she'd taken after Chris ended up in PICU. It was like she burrowed into a ball wrapped in despair. Somehow when he'd kissed her in the elevator, it had pulled her out of that. And straight into his bed. He still wasn't sure how that had happened so fast. He hadn't meant for that to happen. He wasn't so good at relationship stuff.

"So you talked things out?" Angel asked.

Jared turned back to him. "Huh? Oh. More or less."

"Did you talk at all?"

Jared really didn't appreciate the superior attitude coming from the guy who couldn't close the deal, so to speak. "How's it going with Julia?"

"Shut up." Angel stalked over to Julia, said something to her, and she nodded and started out with him.

Emily crossed to him, and the four of them headed for the exit.

"Emily," Angel said, "I heard about your ex on the news with that weird proposal. What happened?"

"Augh," Emily said. "He proposed at my apartment complex. I had to get rid of him and the press."

Jared halted. "What? You didn't tell me that."

"I handled it," Emily said.

Jared ground his teeth. "When did all this happen?"

"Right after I got home from Garner's. That night we went out for drinks."

"Three weeks ago!" he barked.

Angel and Julia exchanged an uneasy look.

"Yeah," Emily said. "I guess it was three weeks ago."

Jared worked hard to rein in his temper. "And you never thought to mention it?"

Dammit. Emily could've been in real danger. She hadn't told him her ex was harassing her. He had no idea the guy was showing up at her place multiple times.

"You never asked," Emily said calmly.

"How would I even know what to ask?" Jared snapped. Their lack of communication was laughable. That was on him. This was exactly why he sucked at relationships. He just couldn't get the hang of all the feelings talk. "You need to file a restraining order," he added.

"I was thinking about it," Emily said. "But I don't think he'd hurt me."

"You should get one," Angel said. "Just to be safe. Don't take that lightly. He seems a little off."

"Honestly I don't think he'll do anything like that again," Emily replied with a glance at Jared. "After the last time, I told him I met someone."

"Why didn't you tell me any of this?" Jared barked. This was all news to him, and he wouldn't have known any of it without Angel and his feelings questions.

"You never asked!" Emily fired back.

"We'll see you later," Angel said before guiding Julia out the door.

"I asked if you were okay," Jared said, figuring he should at least get points for that.

"And I was."

"Why didn't you tell me he kept showing up at your place?"

"Because I handled it. Seriously. Just drop it."

He ground his teeth, mad at her, but also mad at himself for being so caught up in sex that he couldn't have a rational conversation with her the way Angel could. "Sorry I'm not Mr. Feelings Talker like some people."

She gave him a wary look. "Not that again."

"I'm not good at feelings stuff," he said defensively.

"That's okay. I just want you for your body." She sailed out the door.

He followed, feeling like he'd just taken a punch to the gut. That was exactly what he'd suspected, and the truth hurt.

He walked with her back to his truck, silent and sullen. After they were inside, he turned the truck on and blasted the heat. Then he just sat there, struggling for the words that would tell her how much more he wanted than that.

Her gloved hand stroked his hair. "Hey. I was just joking about wanting you for your body. I really like you. Don't be mad."

He turned to look at her. "You like me."

"Sure. You're a lot of fun. I guess I do need fun in my life."

"So it is just for my body."

"Come on. It was a joke!" She gave him a playful punch to the shoulder.

He harrumphed. "Sometimes jokes have a kernel of truth in them."

She waggled her finger at him. "I know what you're doing."

He grabbed her waggling finger. "What am I doing?"

"You're fishing for compliments."

"I—"

"Okay, I'll play. Your eyes are a gorgeous green." She went nose to nose with him and gazed into his eyes.

"Em," he said, the blood rapidly draining from his big head to his little head.

"You taste like spicy sweetness," she said, running her tongue over his bottom lip and then slipping it into his mouth to taste some more. He groaned and cupped the back of her head, kissing her long and deep, unable to stop himself. And then he pulled her on top of his lap, making her straddle him. She rocked her pelvis against him and the rest was a hot blur.

He didn't care that they were in a parking lot.

He didn't care about feelings talk.

He only cared about burying himself deep inside her.

"Em," he managed, that one word both demand and entreaty.

"Yes," she said, quickly undoing his jeans and freeing him. He pushed up her skirt and realized she still had more clothes on under it. "Rip the pantyhose," she said against his mouth.

It was easy to do, with the way she was stretched across him. He slid the panties to the side with one quick move and sank into heaven.

**12**
———

Emily wasn't quite sure how she ended up spending the whole weekend at Jared's place, but somehow she couldn't seem to stop hooking up with him. After the truck hookup—she'd never done anything like that before—he'd driven her straight back to his place, where they'd had some of their Yule log from class. And then Jared got creative with painting her with the cream and licking it off and took her right there on the kitchen table, saying she was his feast. She probably should've left after that, but she'd been tired, and he'd carried her upstairs to bed, his arms warm and strong around her. He'd lulled her into a sated contentment.

Now it was morning, and she knew she really had to go. They'd screwed each other's brains out, and now it was back to reality. She suddenly remembered that weird teddy bear gift and had a moment's hesitation about going home, unsure what might be waiting on her doorstep. It was just a teddy bear, she told herself. Harmless. Probably some neighbor with a crush. Only her gut instinct didn't agree with her brain's rationalization. She pressed her fingers to her temple. What was she supposed to do, move in with Jared out of fear? She wasn't ready for a serious relationship, and she knew very well that wasn't what he was about. He'd told her right up front he had commitment issues, and his rep with the ladies had taken on mythical proportions. Well deserved, but still. She'd be a fool to think he was serious about her.

She glanced over, saw his eyes were closed, and rolled out of bed.

His hand snaked out and grabbed her wrist. "Not so fast."

"Ah!" she yelped.

He pulled her on top of him. They were both still naked from their middle-of-the-night hookup. "I want you," he said, gazing into her eyes.

"I know."

He palmed her ass and squeezed. "A lot."

"I know. I have to go, though."

He rocked her against his hardness. "Every night. I want you in my bed every night."

"You can't have me every night."

He slid his warm hand into her hair and kissed her; she melted against him. Her body overrode her brain whenever he kissed her.

He broke the kiss. "I won't cheat on you," he said out of nowhere.

"Jared, we don't have an exclusive—"

"Yes, exclusive. That's what I want. We should be exclusive."

"I don't even quite know how this weekend happened."

He kissed her again and gazed into her eyes. "It's like…I told you about Jen—"

"Stop!" She tried to roll away, but he pulled her back. "I don't want to hear about your other women," she said through her teeth.

"I'm not talking about sex!"

She throbbed at the word "sex" coming out of his mouth. It was ridiculous how much she wanted him, and she didn't want to talk about Jen or any other women in his past.

He groaned. "Em…you make it so tough to focus on talking."

"What'd I do?" He must've read the desire in her eyes. The need overrode everything else. She kissed his neck and breathed him in, like soap and apple pie and everything good about the world. "We'll talk after."

He rolled on top of her and thrust inside. She moaned loudly and hooked her ankles around his waist. She was already aroused, as he well knew.

He met her eyes. "This weekend happened because…" He pulled nearly all the way out and thrust deep, making her gasp. "You can't resist me."

"I-I…" She couldn't speak as he pumped into her hard and fast and deep. She could feel herself climbing that peak again. "Please."

He pulled nearly all the way out. "Just let me in." His thrust matched his words in a crazy way.

She cried out. "You are in."

He thrust fiercely, and she dug her nails into his back. "More in."

"Oh-oh-oh." He pulled out again, and she grabbed his shoulders to get him back. He slammed back into her, and her breath caught. "You can't go any further in."

He thrust again, and she lifted her hips to take him deeper. They both groaned. "I'm talking about feelings," he said hoarsely when he was buried deep.

"Just fuck me!" She squeezed him with her internal muscles.

He kept going, and she hit a monster peak that shook her to her core and went on and on as he thrust for his own release.

When he finally pulled out, she tried to make her escape, but he was all over her, his hands and mouth immediately dominating all of her hot spots, and she caved again.

He didn't let her go until he was actually sore from too much screwing. She didn't even know that could happen. She could barely walk.

"That is a beautiful thing," he said with a huge ear-to-ear grin after watching her hobble around the room, gathering her clothes and putting them on.

She turned and glared at him. "It's not funny." She was sore in muscles she didn't even know she had.

Jared bounded across the room to where she stood, gave her a quick kiss, and then hauled her back to bed, where he promptly pushed her facedown on the mattress.

"I thought you couldn't screw anymore," she said. Besides, she was fully dressed in her sweater and skirt (sans ripped pantyhose) from the night before.

"The doctor is in," he said before beginning a delicious massage. His large warm hands both relaxed and aroused her as he worked from her neck to her shoulders and back. He moved to her hips, massaging over her skirt, and then around to her bottom. His hands left her for a moment, and she was about to protest that she wanted more when he hiked her skirt up past her hips and moved to more intimate territory. She let him do whatever he wanted because everything he did felt wonderful.

He worked his magic all the way down her legs to her toes and then sent her on her way. She left on a strange high, both euphoric and exhausted from being well used and well handled. She was afraid she was getting addicted to that feeling. Addicted to him.

She knew better than to get attached. He wasn't serious about her. That wasn't his way. Was it? He had said something about feelings in the middle of all that hazy sexy time. But that was just bedroom talk. Right?

She stepped outside and headed to the driveway, where Jared had parked her car, a very safe Volvo sedan. He'd retrieved it from the hospital parking lot late last night, another gesture of good manners, so she was able to drive straight home. Her mind was a confused muddle with all that had happened over the last week—hooking up with Jared for an entire second weekend, Chris fighting for his life in PICU, and the strange gift. She was too overwhelmed and exhausted to make sense of any of it.

When she got home, she stopped short at her door, her hand flying to her mouth. A bouquet of cheerful yellow tulips lay across her welcome mat. They were her favorite flower, but they weren't what Michael usually sent. He always sent roses. Her heart raced as she picked up the bouquet and read the small card with the tiny all caps printed letters: *You are very pretty. I want to see you more.* The phrasing was odd to her ears. Unfamiliar. Maybe a teenager in the apartment complex who liked to watch her? She shuddered.

She darted a quick look around, saw no one, and rushed inside. She called Jared. "Did you send me flowers?"

"Em? You okay?"

"Yes. No. Did you send me flowers?"

"No. Was there a card?"

"Yes! I know to look for a card!"

"Okay, calm down. Tell me what it said."

She told him, and then she told him about the teddy bear.

"I don't like this," he said, an edge to his voice. She felt marginally better it wasn't just her freaking out for no good reason.

She dropped the flowers in the garbage, stopped, and retrieved the card for evidence in case her admirer turned out to be a murderer. Yup, she was that freaked out. "Maybe I have a secret admirer around the apartment complex. Maybe it's a teenager with a crush."

"You should call the cops just to get it on record. You want me to come over?"

"No, I'm fine," she said even though she was shaken up. She didn't want to depend on Jared too much. He wasn't going to stick around. She knew that.

"I'm coming over," he said and hung up.

Monday morning Emily said goodbye to Jared as he left for a meeting at the hospital. They had only slept last night in bed and, strange as it was, she actually slept better than she had in a really long time. Something about his calm demeanor, his easygoing joking manner, made her relax even with all the stress in her life. Last night he'd gone with her to the police station, where they showed the odd gifts to Chief O'Hare. The officer had filed a report, but warned them there was nothing the police could do unless the person took action against her. At least there was a record of it. Jared offered to stay at her place (or vice versa) for as long as she wanted, until she felt safe again, but she knew that would be a mistake. Too serious, too soon for both of them.

An hour later, she left for work, turning to make sure the door was securely locked behind her, and froze. A note taped to the door read—in a red, angry scrawl—*SLUT*.

She sucked in air, the ugly word terrifying her. Someone knew Jared had spent the night with her. It was the first time he'd spent the night. That meant it was either someone who lived in the apartment complex or someone was camped out nearby watching her. Would Michael really go that far? Try to scare her and then swoop in to reassure her? Was it someone she knew or some wacked-out stranger?

She grabbed the paper and drove straight to the Clover Park police station with this latest bit of evidence and handed it over to the officer on duty. Her day just got worse from there. When she got to work, she was met with the news that Chris was on a ventilator, the machine breathing for him, and had slipped into a coma. Some part of him had already left this world. It seemed death was not far off.

The day was grueling as she hustled through her work and made several trips up to PICU to check in on Chris. Tony, Chris's dad, begged her to stay every time. She did all that she could, visiting as much as she could, calling in a priest to console Tony, bringing food to him. It was a terrible, terrible thing for a parent to watch their child on their deathbed.

She left work, frazzled and on edge. And found Michael on her doorstep.

She screamed bloody murder.

"Emily! What's wrong?"

She nearly tripped over herself as she whirled and ran for the stairs, her heart in her throat. She raced down the stairs and back to her Volvo.

"Emily, wait!"

Her hands were shaking, but she managed to open the car door. She heard footsteps as Michael took the stairs, hurrying to catch up with her. Her purse strap snagged on the door as she tried to get in, and she wrestled with it frantically.

"I've been wanting to see you," Michael said. She glanced up to see he was at the bottom of the stairs. *Oh, God. Why hadn't she gone through with the restraining order?* She got the strap free, slammed the door, and locked herself in. She turned the car on and yelped at a sharp knock on her window.

Michael stood there, looking in at her with an oddly determined expression on his face.

"Back off!" she shouted through the glass before putting the car in reverse and making a quick acceleration straight back. Michael stepped away from the car. She sped out of the lot and drove like Satan himself was on her tail all the way to the police station.

She burst inside and blurted out everything to the officer on duty. He left to check on her apartment, and she waited at the station with the secretary, Linda, a kindly woman in her sixties with curly red hair. Fifteen minutes later, the officer reported back that no one was at her apartment.

"He was there," she told Linda. "I'm not crazy."

Linda gave her a gentle smile. "Do you have someone I could call to be with you, sweetie?"

She scrunched her eyes shut tight at the tears that threatened. She knew she shouldn't be alone right now. She nodded.

Jared was there in ten minutes flat. No questions asked.

Jared woke early the next morning with a naked Emily in his bed. They still hadn't talked things out, but she'd called him in her moment of need, and that had to mean something. He had to at least try to get the words out. She meant more to him than a hookup. A lot more. He spooned her from behind and started kissing her neck. A few minutes later, she hooked her leg over his and reached back to run her fingers through his hair.

"You've turned me into a sex addict," she said, her voice still rough from sleep. "I just woke up, and I want you so bad."

It occurred to him he was a little too good at what he did. He'd tried to get the feelings thing across, but it kept getting effed up. Literally. Maybe he should go in the other direction. Hands off. She ground her shapely bottom back against his erection, and he groaned and held her snug against him.

Okay, so hands off was *not* an option. Should he blurt out the L word? Because the more he was with her, the more it felt true. But what if she didn't L back? He'd be F'd for sure.

"I told you I want you every night," he said in a low voice near her ear. "And here you are."

She dropped her arm from him. "This was a fluke. I had a horrible day yesterday."

He ran a hand up and down her leg, trying to slow things down enough to speak coherently. "I don't just mean to sleep with you. I mean, you know, regular kind of sleeping too."

She took his hand and moved it to her breasts. "Do that thing you do."

He kept his hand still. "We should go out to dinner. Like dating." *Like a relationship.* Though, he couldn't quite get the word "relationship" out. At least he could think it now.

She turned in his arms to face him. "I don't want to go out to dinner. I like this better." She grabbed his head, pulled him down, and kissed him. He kissed her back, his body urging him to take her. No, he had to get through to her.

He pulled back. "Here's what I want to say…" And then nothing came out. *Dammit.* He still didn't have the right words. He was afraid to blurt too much and then have it just hanging out there, unreturned.

She threw an arm and leg around him. "What?"

"I have, like…" *A lot of feelings. Maybe the L kind.* "You know how I told you about Jen?"

Her brown eyes flashed at him. "Would you stop bringing up your ex-girlfriend!"

"I'm trying to explain feelings!"

"What do you need her for?"

"Because I lived with her and then she left and it was hard. But I want to take a chance again. With you."

Her eyes widened. "Are you trying to say you're serious about me?"

"As a heart attack."

"I thought…I guess I thought we were just having fun?"

He rolled to his back and stared at the ceiling.

"Jare, I'm never getting married again."

"Who said anything about marriage?" Though it was surprisingly hard to hear that.

She sat up. "Sorry. I misspoke. I just meant I don't want to get serious with any guy again."

"So it's not just me."

"Exactly."

He looked at her, nearly breathless at her beauty as her glossy brown hair cascaded over her bare shoulders. Her beautiful full breasts that he was aching to touch. "Okay," he said slowly. "So what does that mean for us?"

She blew out a breath. "I don't know. I figured eventually you'd get tired of me."

He frowned. "What if I don't?"

She was quiet.

"Wait a minute." He sat up. "You mean eventually *you'll* get tired of *me*. That's what you're really trying to say."

She turned away. "Don't go putting words in my mouth. I'm just trying to be practical."

"Yeah? Well, practical sucks."

Her expression softened as she turned back to him. "Don't make this more complicated than it needs to be. Okay?" She kissed him and ran her hands over his shoulders and chest, working him up.

"Em…I…" He sucked in a breath as her hand trailed lower. He took over in a fierce possession that told her what his words couldn't. His mouth claimed hers as he rolled her under him. He lifted his head. "You put down the gauntlet, and I'm picking it up."

Her cheeks flushed pink. "There's no gauntlet. I just need to keep things light. Okay?"

He nipped her bottom lip. "I'm gonna wear you down." She moaned as he started working his way down her body, kissing and tasting as he went.

"Jare?" she asked in a breathy voice. "You heard what I said?"

He reached her stomach. "Open those legs for me, darling."

She did. He was lost. So was she. There was nothing but this woman and what she made him feel, which was insanely good.

**13**

———

Emily worked with quiet despair as it became apparent over the next two days that Chris was only getting worse. Even Jared couldn't bring her out of her funk, though he tried, showing up at her apartment every night, bringing her take-out, watching TV with her, holding her close. She couldn't turn him away even if it was a mistake to let him in close. She was too distraught, and his calm presence steadied her.

Thursday night Chris passed away.

She got the call from the on-duty nurse, who knew she wanted to hear. It wasn't a shock. The child had suffered for years, but still the news devastated her. Jared was with her when she got the call.

He wrapped his arms around her, offering comfort. "What can I do?"

"I just need to be alone right now."

"Are you sure?"

She pulled away and dashed at her eyes, scrubbing away the few tears that had escaped. "Please."

"Em, you don't have to do this alone. I miss him too. He was a good kid." His voice broke, and she couldn't handle both of them losing it. "A real good kid."

"I need some space." She headed to her bedroom and shut the door behind her.

A few moments later, she heard the front door open and then quietly shut.

She sobbed uncontrollably until she had no tears left, her eyes dry and gritty. And then she crawled under the covers, knowing she'd have to return to work tomorrow for the other patients' sake. It always shook up the children when they heard a fellow patient was gone. At least she finally felt safe at home again. Ever since she'd gone to the police about Michael showing up at her place, the gifts had stopped. She hadn't seen or heard from Michael either.

She returned to work on Friday only to meet up with a distraught Tony, Chris's father. His clothes were wrinkled, his hair disheveled, and his eyes were red from too much crying.

"He's gone," he choked out before breaking down and sobbing.

She gently guided him to the break room and settled with him on the sofa. The two nurses on break quickly left, giving them privacy.

"I have nothing," Tony said. "Chris was my whole world."

"I'm so sorry."

"He was such a good boy. I did my best with him. If only his mom hadn't died." The man dropped his head in his hands and sobbed some more. "Why?" he wailed. "Why couldn't it have been me?"

Emily didn't know what to say. There was never any good reason for a child to have a disease. It was unfair, plain and simple. "I'm so sorry," she kept saying as he got all of his anger and frustration out over the unfairness of it all.

Eventually he calmed down enough to say, "Tell me a story about him. About your time with him."

"He loved baseball. He knew all the stats on all the Yankees."

"That was our team. I took him to the games before he got...too bad."

"He often spoke about the autographed Derek Jeter card you got him."

"Jeter's a real class act," he said, wiping his eyes with the back of his hand.

They spent some time reminiscing about Chris, and Emily confessed she wished she'd been there the weekend he ended up in PICU.

"I wish you'd been there too," Tony said. "You were his good luck charm. He kept hanging on, kept fighting."

"I'm sure he hung on because he was strong. Not because of me."

His voice became hard. "It sure didn't help that you weren't there for him."

"I'm so sorry," she said. "I still feel terrible about that."

His eyes filled again. "Too late now." He broke down in tears, and she tried to comfort him as best she could. He clung to her arm. She was really late for her shift, knew she had to check on the other patients, but Tony's grip on her arm was so tight.

"I need to go back to work," she said gently. "Would you like me to call a priest or a social worker?"

"I just want you. You're the one who knew him best. You're the one who cared about him. None of these other people could give a shit that we lost the best soul on earth." His voice turned angry, his fingers pressing painfully into her arm. "Why weren't you there for him?"

"You're hurting me."

He dropped his hand and started pacing the small space, muttering to himself.

"Tony, I'm so sorry. I know this is such…" She trailed off at the alarming look in his eyes as he stopped pacing and glared at her, the vein in his forehead bulging.

"Why weren't you at your post that day?" he thundered.

Guilt swamped her. She wished she had been. "They did everything they could for him," she said quietly.

He marched over to her and got in her face. "What were you so busy doing that was more important than saving a life!" he hollered, spittle coming out of his mouth.

She took a careful step back. "Let me call someone."

"Chris needed you!" he raged. "And you weren't there!"

"I—"

Her supervisor, Jane, popped her head in the door. "Everything okay in here?"

Tony headed toward the door, nearly knocking Jane over as he rushed out. Emily took in a shaky breath.

"That man needs to talk to psych," Jane said. "You know you're supposed to call them when we lose a patient."

"I thought I could help him," she said in a small voice. She shook her head. "He always seemed to feel better talking to me."

"That's not your job," Jane said. "You can't be everything to everyone."

"The man just lost his son!" Emily snapped. "We're just supposed to step back and let a stranger console him? I knew Chris better than anyone here. Tony knew that, and he needed me."

"Sometimes the grieving need more than us. Sometimes they need a professional to help them cope."

Emily shook her head and went back to work, knowing she could never be hands-off like that with her young patients and their families.

When she finally finished her shift, every nerve felt scraped raw. She headed to the parking lot and stopped short. Jared was standing next to her car. She couldn't deal with more emotional upheaval.

"Em," he said, holding his arms out to her, "c'mere."

Her eyes welled again, and she bit her lip hard. She had to get home before she fell apart.

"You want to come to my place?" he asked. "I can order some takeout. Or I can come to yours?"

"I can't," she said on a sob.

He pulled her in for a tight hug, and she sobbed into his fleece jacket. He stroked her hair. After a few moments, he spoke gently. "If you don't want me to come over, do you have someone else you can call? A friend? Some family?"

She backed away. "I told you I just need to be alone."

"You shouldn't be alone right now."

She skirted past him and opened the car door. "You don't understand." She got in and drove away.

The grief was overwhelming, the guilt over what she could've done, what she should've done just about killed her. Poor Tony. He was the one who really suffered. She hadn't been there when her patient needed her most, and now he was gone.

~

Jared went to the hospital the very next morning for his usual Saturday Captain Huddle visit. The kids needed him now more than ever. He met up with Emily, who had dark circles under her brown eyes, her fair skin pale and sallow. He was beyond worried about her. She'd shut him out, shut everyone out, it seemed, in her grief.

"Are you feeling okay?" he asked, pressing the back of his hand to her forehead, automatically checking her vitals. No fever.

She pushed his hand away. "I haven't been sleeping very well." She handed him the goody bag. "Thank you for coming. It's important to the kids."

"Of course." He pushed up his eye mask. "How are—"

"Emily!" a man's voice boomed.

They turned at the same time to a thirty-something bulky man with a wild look in his eyes. His dark brown hair was messy, his clothes wrinkled like he'd slept in them.

"Who's that?" Jared asked. His senses went on full alert. There was something unstable about the man that made him wary.

"It's Chris's dad," Emily said quietly. "I'll handle this. He just needs to talk. The funeral is today at noon."

He watched as Emily headed toward the man. She'd only taken two steps when the man pulled a gun.

Jared swung into motion. "Drop the gun!" he hollered as he charged ahead, knocking Emily sideways to the ground and barreling straight toward the man.

The gun pointed at him now, and he dove for the man's waist, slamming him to the ground. His shoulder burned as he wrestled the man until he had him pinned and managed to pry the gun out of the man's clenched fist. He tossed the gun with a low push across the linoleum floor and pinned both the man's wrists over his head as he held him down with one knee in his chest. "Call security!"

Only moments later, security arrived and cuffed the man, taking him away.

"Jared," Emily said in a voice that sounded very far away, "you're bleeding. You were shot. We need to get you to emergency."

Someone showed up with a wheelchair.

He stared at the wheelchair. "I'm fine." He looked himself over and saw a puddle of blood on the floor. The burning in his shoulder was now a dull ache. Emily was pressing a pile of gauze against his shoulder. In his adrenaline rush, he hadn't even felt the shot, hadn't heard it, all he could focus on was taking the dangerous man down.

He looked down at her. "I'm fine. Really. Damn, I ruined the costume."

Her voice came out shaky. "You saved me. I can't believe you risked your life for me."

"I had to," he said before he got light-headed and couldn't speak. Someone pushed him to the wheelchair. He must've lost more blood than he realized. He drifted into unconsciousness. He came to on a cot in the emergency room, all bandaged up with his arm in a sling. Emily sat by his side, holding the hat and mask from his costume.

"What's going on?" he asked.

"Jared!" Her eyes were shiny with tears.

"Don't cry, I'll be fine." He grimaced because his shoulder hurt like hell. "How bad is it?"

"The bullet didn't go all the way through. They want to take you to X-ray to see where it's lodged."

"Okay."

"Oh, Jared!" She started sobbing. He wished he could hug her, but he was afraid to move because of the awful pain in his shoulder.

"It's bad luck to cry in front of a patient," he said instead.

She immediately wiped her eyes and bit her lip, nodding.

He liked that she pulled herself together for his sake. She probably did that for all her patients, always looking out for their best interests. It only made him love her more. Whoa. He really did. He had to let her know. She needed someone to be there for her at the end of the day after being there for everyone else.

"Em, I…uh…I…" *Dammit.* Why couldn't he get the words out?

"What is it?" she asked. "What do you need?"

"We're ready to take you to X-ray now," a nurse said. He blew out a breath of relief. He needed more time to figure out what to say. And some assurance that she felt the same way.

A short while later it was clear he'd need arthroscopic surgery because the bullet was lodged in the joint. He'd been damn lucky. It had just missed his artery. He was already scheduled for Monday afternoon with a good surgeon. They wheeled him to a private room to speak to the police. Emily was there.

"What'd they say?" she asked.

"Just a little arthroscopic surgery." He'd have to reschedule all of his patients. He had three to four surgeries every Wednesday. "I'll be out of commission at least a month. My patients—"

"You're the patient now," she said firmly. "We'll refer the emergencies and the others will have to wait." She pushed his hair back and kissed his forehead. "Thank you for saving my life."

"I told you I'm the idiot always running toward danger. What happened to the guy with the gun?"

"He's with the psychiatrist right now. I signed a restraining order to keep him from me and the hospital. He's not in his right mind, but I can't help but feel for him. I don't want to press charges."

"He'll still pay for what he did. He put everyone at risk bringing a gun into the hospital. What if he'd hit one of the patients?"

"Why are you so calm?" she asked.

"I don't know. Maybe it's the blood loss. Maybe I'm just used to dealing with emergencies. I sort of live for this shit."

"Oh, Jared," she said on a sob.

"You're making me feel like I'm dying." He sent a pleading look to the police officer waiting patiently nearby.

"I'm Officer Kent, Eastman P.D. If I could have a word?"

Emily took Jared's hand, completely ignoring the officer. "I'm going to nurse you back to health. It's the least I can do."

He smiled. "That sounds real good."

Jared answered the officer's questions, describing what happened as best he remembered it. The officer turned to Emily. "Mr. Messina stated he didn't intend to shoot you or anyone else. He wanted you to see him kill himself. That was his plan."

Jared clenched his jaw. The man wanted her to live with that on her conscience.

"He wanted me to suffer for not being there for Chris," Emily said softly.

"Are you sure you don't want to press charges?" the officer asked.

Emily hesitated and stared at the ground, her forehead crinkled like she was trying to decide.

He watched her for a moment when something occurred to him. "Are you thinking about those strange gifts?"

She lifted her gaze to his, her lips parted in surprise. "Yes."

"What gifts?" Officer Kent asked. He was an Eastman cop, not Clover Park, so he didn't know about Emily's stalker.

Emily quickly filled him in.

Officer Kent nodded. "The perp often uses printed capital letters to disguise his writing. Don't worry. We can still analyze it. Might find some fingerprints too."

Emily nodded. "Okay, if it was Tony, I will be pressing charges. That's above and beyond a grieving father."

The officer thanked them both and left.

Jared thought Tony already was beyond the range of a normal grieving father—the look in his eyes was terrifying, both furious and dead calm. But Jared let it go for now because there were still other charges being brought against Tony. He was a risk both to himself and others. Right now all he cared about was Emily being at his side, exactly where she belonged.

Emily pushed Jared's wheelchair out of the hospital exit and was met by a swarm of reporters. Her ex-husband, Michael, stood right out front wearing a suit, apparently waiting for her.

Michael rushed over and enveloped her in a hug. "Emily, thank God you're okay."

She fought his embrace, her heart thundering against her rib cage. "Don't touch me!" She still didn't know if Michael was the one responsible for the anonymous gifts and ugly note.

"Back off," Jared growled, and Michael dropped his hands.

Emily looked around frantically for an exit. Jared looked at her over his shoulder and winced from the movement. "You okay back there?"

She moved close to his side and whispered in his ear, "What if it's Michael who left those creepy gifts?"

Jared narrowed his eyes and turned to Michael just as her ex announced grandly for all of the news reporters to hear, "Thank you, Dr. Reynolds, for your help with my Emily. We're both so grateful for your heroic efforts."

Emily stepped behind Jared's wheelchair, her hands tight on the handles in case they needed to make a fast escape.

The press closed in, their questions rapid-fire:

"Did you know the shooter?"

"Dr. Reynolds, can you tell us what happened?"

"Was this shooting over a love triangle?"

"Love triangle!" Jared barked. "Emily is with me."

"I've never felt closer to Emily," Michael said, his chest puffing up. He stood in front of Jared. "And I'm sure she'd have to agree—"

Jared shot out his foot, connecting with the back of Michael's knee, causing him to tumble forward. All of it on film.

Emily pulled Jared's wheelchair back as Michael bounded to his feet and whirled on Jared, rage making his cheeks a mottled red.

A surge of protective instinct rushed through Emily. "Enough!"

Everyone fell silent.

Michael straightened his tie and seemed to recover himself as he once again pasted on a pleasant face for the cameras.

Emily spoke loud and clear. "I ended my marriage two years ago, and there will never be a reconciliation. What Michael did was unforgiveable."

"I apologized," Michael said, looking first to her and then to the press.

Emily held up a hand. "Here's what you need to know. Dr. Jared Reynolds is a true hero, who sacrificed himself for the safety of me, the children in the ward, and our staff."

"Can you tell us more about the shooter?" a reporter asked.

"He was a distraught father who recently lost his son," she said. "That's all I will say out of respect for the family's privacy. Now, if you'll excuse me, I'm going to nurse this hero back to health."

She leaned down and kissed Jared on the cheek. He grinned. Flashes went off as cameras captured the moment. Some video cameras would surely put them on the news as well. She wheeled him to her car and, though some reporters followed them, she had no further comment. If there was one good thing her scandalous past could offer her, it was this experience in dealing effectively with the press.

Michael stayed behind, watching them go.

A short drive later, Emily pulled up to Jared's house, where a bunch of cars were already parked in the driveway and in front of the house. "Do you recognize these cars?" She feared more press were camped out at his house.

"The cavalry has arrived," he said with a smile. "I called

home earlier to tell them I was okay. I'm the second youngest, so they probably want to baby me."

It suddenly occurred to her that he didn't need her at all. She'd been imagining nursing him back to health. It was the least she could do after he risked his life for her.

"So, I guess I'll just let them do their thing," she said, pulling up behind a silver Tesla.

Jared turned to her. "Stay."

"You sure?"

"I'm sure."

Soon Jared was camped out on the sofa with a glass of water and some homemade Italian soup with meatballs and endive.

"A very healing recipe," Mrs. Marino proclaimed before insisting Emily enjoy the same. She sat by Jared's side and took her bowl of soup.

His family—his parents and all of his brothers and sisters-in-law—peppered him with questions, often speaking over each other and causing a loud ruckus. Jared took it in stride, seeming to enjoy being the center of attention as he told them his version of the story, which was actually pretty modest, so she had to interrupt a few times to let everyone know just how brave he really was.

"We knew you were our clutch player," Vince boomed. "Damn, Jare, I don't know what we'd do if..." He trailed off, wiping at his eyes. Everyone got quiet. His wife, Sophia, wrapped her arms around him, hugging him from the side.

"Nah," Jared said, breaking the silence. "I always pull through."

"How long are you going to be in a sling?" Luke asked.

"I've got surgery scheduled on Monday—"

"Surgery!" Angel exclaimed. "That sounds serious."

"Yeah," everyone agreed.

Jared took a spoonful of soup. "It's arthroscopic. Small incision. Only a month recovery. Normally they'd just leave the bullet in and let the tissue grow around it, but it's in the joint, so better to get it out."

His family fussed over him for a while until Jared's eyes became heavy, and he slumped back on the sofa.

"We should go," Mrs. Marino said. "Will you be staying?" she asked Emily.

"Yes."

"Good. I'm sure as a nurse you'll know exactly what to do." She hugged Emily, surprising her because she was, after all, the reason Jared had almost gotten killed.

"I'm very sorry about all of this," Emily said.

"Not at all," Mrs. Marino said. "None of this was your fault. You're just a good person caught in difficult circumstances. Call me if you need anything."

"Okay," she managed over the lump in her throat.

Each of his brothers stopped to give her their card with their cell numbers on it. His oldest brother, Gabe, insisted she call about her legal rights. He wanted to make sure Mr. Messina couldn't ever cause such a dangerous situation again.

After everyone left and the house was quiet, she turned to Jared. He'd fallen asleep, half slumped over. She gently guided him to a more comfortable position, fetched a blanket, and covered him with it.

Then she sat on the floor next to him and finally let herself feel all the terror—the fear for her own life and the near miss for Jared—and broke down in tears. When the tears were spent, she tucked her legs to the side and leaned her cheek against Jared's leg, needing to be close.

She thought again of Tony. The way he wanted her to suffer for not being there for Chris. Normally she would've taken that to heart, but she was done blaming herself for things out of her control. She couldn't have known Chris would end up in PICU. She had to be gentler with herself. She wasn't an awful person. It was like Jared's mom said, she was just a good person caught in difficult circumstances. She really wanted to believe that. She *needed* to believe that. Some difficult circumstances, like working with terminally ill children, she'd freely accepted on her own, some were forced upon her like with her ex and his scandal. In any case, it was time to believe that she deserved happiness.

She closed her eyes as the exhaustion of the day caught up with her and drifted off to sleep.

She woke with a start to the sound of her cell ringing and leaped up to answer it before it woke Jared. She fumbled through her purse and answered quickly. "Hello?"

"Is this Emily Maguire?" an unfamiliar male voice asked.

She gripped the phone tighter and kept her voice low. "Who is this?"

"Officer Kent. We spoke earlier."

Relief flooded her. She hadn't recognized him right away in her exhaustion. "Yes, hello."

"We didn't need to wait on fingerprints. Mr. Messina has been telling everyone all about you and the gifts he gave you. His description matches the evidence you turned in earlier."

She bit her lip, strangely relieved and sad and heartbroken all at the same time. The cancer had broken him. Or maybe he was always broken. Either way it was disturbing.

The officer went on. "We'll need you to sign a few papers when you can get into the station. Mr. Messina is heavily sedated and is no further danger to you."

"Okay, thank you. I'll stop by tomorrow."

She hung up, and in that moment everything became clear. Life was too short, and the only thing that mattered was grabbing love with both hands when that rare, true thing unexpectedly struck, no matter the risk to your heart.

She turned to find Jared's green eyes open and staring at her.

"What happened?" Jared asked when Emily reached his side.

She fussed with the blanket. "You want to sit up?"

"I got it." He levered himself to a sitting position and winced as his shoulder was jostled with the movement.

"Take it easy," she said. "Slow and steady. I'll get your medicine."

He grunted. He was due for more of the pain medication. Of course she'd take good care of him. She was a nurse. But who the hell was that on the phone? That better not have been her ex. He felt like pounding his face in. Even if he passed out from the pain in his shoulder, it would be worth it.

She returned, and he swallowed the pills. "Who called?" he asked.

She sat next to him on the sofa and took his hand on his uninjured side. "The police. Officer Kent confirmed it was Tony leaving those strange gifts. I'm pressing charges. Tomorrow I'll sign the papers."

"It's over," Jared said, giving her hand a squeeze. "Smooth sailing from here on out."

She gave him a small smile. "After the day you had, I can't believe you're looking for the sunny side."

"You're my sunny side," he said gruffly.

"Oh, Jared," she said, her voice catching on his name. "I realized something about our relationship—"

"We have a relationship now?" He had to ask because they never did have that important feelings talk.

"If you want one. I know I do."

"So that's all it took, huh? Taking a bullet for you."

She gazed up at him tenderly. "It took me realizing why you risked your life for me."

He raised a brow. "Oh, yeah? Why do you think?"

"Because you love me." She smiled sweetly.

"You sure about that?" *And do you love me back?*

"That's why you kept bringing up Jen, the first woman you loved. That's why you said your heart couldn't take it when I wanted to fool around some more on our ski weekend. Your heart was involved. I've never been just a hookup to you."

He grunted. "Took you long enough to catch on."

She smiled warmly. "You weren't the easiest person to read, especially given your rep."

"You're easy enough to read. You just wanted me for my body."

She laughed and then unexpectedly cried.

"Hey, I'm sorry," he said. "I always seem to go too far with the joking."

"No, it's fine. I love you for more than your body, I promise."

"What do you love me for?" he asked, fishing for compliments.

"I love you for your good nature, for your compassion, for your willingness to do for others, for your thoughtfulness—"

"Wow. And not one mention of my biceps."

"I love those too." She kissed his bicep.

"I love you." He kissed her tenderly. "And I'm glad we both lived long enough to realize that. God, Em. I couldn't have lived with myself if anything had happened to you."

"I feel the same way about you."

He looked down into her beautiful face and knew deep down this was what he'd been waiting for all of his bachelor years. The woman that made him feel like he'd finally found home. "I'm going to need a lot of care after my surgery."

She smiled, her eyes shiny with unshed tears and love. He saw that clear as day. "I'll be there."

He wrapped an arm around her, and they stayed like that for a long time, holding each other as well as they could with his injury. A calm settled over him. True love could do that to a guy.

**14**
———

Emily headed to the Marino-Reynolds Christmas Eve celebra-tion at Gabe's house the next week in a merry mood. Jared's surgery had gone well, and he was back to his normal teasing, good-natured, sexy self. She'd planned to spend the week fussing over him, but between his family and Jared's own insistence on keeping some work hours to follow up on patients, she hadn't gotten much chance. At least she'd had some time to make him a Christmas gift.

After a feast of several seafood courses—clams, spaghetti with mussels, shrimp marsala, and even baked eel—the family migrated to the large kitchen for dessert. Their dog, Fred, hadn't been tempted by the feast because he was too busy in the corner, chewing on a cow hoof he'd received as an early Christmas present.

Emily was a little surprised after all the dinner courses to find only one dessert—a huge platter of crescent cookies covered in powdered sugar. Mrs. Marino offered the cookies to Emily first because she was the guest. She took one and then watched as Mrs. Marino offered one to Jared with a big smile. He ate it in two bites.

Everyone cheered, startling Emily.

"Italian wedding cookies," Sophia explained, though Emily

had no idea why they'd be having wedding cookies on Christmas Eve. "She also got you to eat the Italian wedding soup. That's what the healing meatball soup was at Jared's house."

Emily's brows drew together. "I'm confused. Is this because Luke's engaged?"

"Nope!" Luke said with a big grin, putting his arm around his fiancée, Kennedy.

"There's only one thing to do," Jared said, going down on one knee in front of her.

Emily clapped a hand over her mouth as her eyes filled with happy tears.

"Where's the ring, Doc?" Vince asked.

Jared made a face. "I'll get one later."

Sophia rushed over and tried to take hers off. "It's stuck!" she wailed. "My fingers are too swollen." She was fifteen weeks along with her pregnancy, as Vince had informed them all earlier, and over her morning sickness.

Kennedy tried next, pulling her huge diamond engagement ring off.

"Hey!" Luke protested. "That's yours."

"It's temporary," Kennedy replied.

Jared tried to slide it on Emily's finger, but it was too small.

Lily crossed to them where Jared was still down on one knee. She pulled her small diamond ring off and handed it to Jared, smiling at them both. "I have another ring." She pointed to a small turquoise ring on her other hand. "It was Nico's mom's ring and means more than any diamond to me."

This was significant, Emily knew, because Nico's mom had died when he was just a kid, and Lily was the wealthy Spencer heiress.

"Aww, Lil," Nico said. She crossed to him, and he wrapped his arms around her, kissing her red hair.

Jared held up the diamond ring to Emily. "Will you let me be your good-for-you guy?"

"He always was!" Angel put in.

"Ignore him," Jared said, shooting Angel a dark look. "Damn interloper."

She grinned and whispered, "Will you still be my good-time guy too?"

"Yes." He lowered his voice. "Five and never done."

They grinned at each other.

"Uh, Jare, you never actually asked her," Angel pointed out.

"Emily, will you marry me?" Jared asked grandly.

She nodded through tears. He slipped the ring onto her finger. She dropped to her knees and hugged him.

"Watch the shoulder," Jared said on a groan.

"I'm sorry!" she cried. "I love you so much."

"I love you too so much," Jared said, and then they were kissing.

"Damn, Ma, those cookies are scary strong," Vince observed.

"What about the cookies?" Emily asked, dashing tears from her eyes.

Jared stood, and she did too. "It's some voodoo magic my mom puts into those Italian wedding cookies. Every one of my brothers and their girlfriends ate them and then ended up getting married."

"Except us," Zoe said, hitching a thumb at her husband, Gabe. "We got pregnant."

"Which one will it be for you, Angel?" Mrs. Marino asked.

Angel ran a hand through his hair. "Ah, I'm the exception that proves the rule."

"Not if I can help it," Mrs. Marino and Jared said at the same time.

"Watch out, Angel!" Vince boomed. "They got it in for you."

"Bring it on," Angel said with a devilish grin.

Everyone laughed. Then they all gathered around her and Jared, congratulating them and welcoming her to the family. She was having a hard time keeping it together, so overwhelmed with the outpouring of love. She kept crying and apologizing for her tears until Angel stopped her.

"Hey, don't apologize for your feelings," Angel said. "We're all thrilled that you're happy to be part of the family. And if that comes out in tears, we're all good with that. Right, guys?"

The women agreed. The men snickered. "Right, Saint Angel," Vince said.

"Just Angel," Jared said. "He's no saint."

"He's no angel either," Emily put in with a grin.

Jared leaned down to her ear. "I'm the only guy you're going to be naughty with."

"Ooo-hoo-hoo!" Luke crowed. "Jared's getting naughty."

"I really hope this will end the fighting between you two," Mrs. Marino said, looking to Jared and Angel.

"Then what'll we bet on?" Nico asked.

"Who'll get pregnant next, Emily, Kennedy, or Zoe!" Vince proclaimed, causing a murmur among the men as they eyed the women in the room who could be in contention.

"Inappropriate," Mr. Marino intoned, and the brothers quickly hushed with their betting.

Emily's cheeks burned. "Gosh, this was all such a surprise, I—ah!"

Jared had yanked her out of the room. He led her around the corner to the living room, where he kissed her in an erotic reminder of just who she was going to have all her naughty times with from now on or maybe just who was going to get pregnant next. She didn't know and it didn't matter. All that mattered was him.

He pressed his forehead to hers. "I'm so glad you said yes," he said in a choked voice.

She broke down in tears. "Of course I said yes."

He wiped her tears with his thumb and kissed her again. "I'll be good for you, I promise."

"I know you will. You always were."

He kissed her again; the kiss turned heated, more demanding. And then she was against the wall, and he was pressing against her. She couldn't believe how much she wanted him even knowing his entire family was mere feet away.

He shifted and kissed along her neck. "I wish we were alone right now."

"Me too."

"After presents." He'd told her they opened gifts at midnight, so that gave them the whole night after that. He lifted his head and gazed into her eyes. "All I want for Christmas is you," he said gruffly.

"Jared," she said in a teasing voice, "I had no idea you were so good with words." The line was straight out of a popular Christmas song.

He tugged a lock of her hair playfully. "I thought all my 'uh' and 'um' and Jen talk was pretty clear. Obviously I loved you with all my heart and wanted a committed relationship."

"Yes, I got that right away."

He barked out a laugh. "I got the same vibe from you when you begged for an orgasm."

"Shh! Keep your voice down!"

One corner of his mouth lifted. "What'll you give me?"

She grinned. "Whatever you want."

He lifted her hand with the temporary engagement ring and kissed the back of her fingers. "I have all I want."

"Listen to you, Mr. Romantic! Swoon!"

"That's Dr. Romantic."

"I like that nickname a lot better than your old one."

"Me too." He looked around. "Where's a supply closet when you need one?"

She threw her arms around his neck and kissed him passionately. He tore his mouth from hers and whispered urgently in her ear, "I can't wait. Follow me."

She nodded. He put a finger to his mouth in a shushing motion. She quietly followed him through a nearby door that led to a basement made into a man cave with a home theater and pool table. He led her to the pool table, shut off the light, and returned to her.

"We have to be absolutely silent," he whispered as he yanked her skirt up past her waist.

"You're going to have to muffle me," she said, sliding her tights and panties down. She made quick work of his pants and briefs before taking him in hand. He groaned and flipped her around, pushing her down over the table.

"Like this?" he asked, putting a hand over her mouth as he thrust inside.

"Yes!" she exclaimed against his hand, half in relief.

He grunted and the only sound was their bodies slapping together, her muffled gasps and moans, and then a low guttural groan that shook them both up as they raced over the edge together.

After, she was embarrassed. She yanked her clothes back in place. "Do you think they'll know? We should've waited."

"Nah. Everyone's busy talking in the kitchen. No one will even notice we were gone."

They stealthily made their way back upstairs, emerged through the door that led back to the living room, and Fred barked like crazy, giving them away. Unfortunately, all of Jared's brothers and sisters-in-law were gathered in the living room around the Christmas tree. At least Mr. and Mrs. Marino weren't there. They probably got stuck with dishes duty.

"Taking the edge off?" Angel asked with a smirk.

Everyone laughed. Emily was mortified. "Jared was just teaching me how to play pool."

"Did he get one in the corner pocket?" Luke asked.

"Who broke first?" Gabe asked.

"Did you polish the shaft?" Vince asked.

"I really hope you didn't snooker," Nico said with a grin.

"Emily got the money ball," Jared announced. "'Nuf said."

His brothers laughed and slapped him on the back.

"Jared!" Emily exclaimed, not used to all the teasing.

"It means you won," he said with a straight face.

She smoothed her hair. "Oh."

His brothers kept chuckling and ribbing Jared, so she made her escape to hang out with the women standing nearby.

"They're so obnoxious, aren't they?" Sophia asked.

"Yes," Emily said, glad to have someone on her side.

"But so irresistible," Lily said on a sigh, looking over at Nico.

"Totally," Emily said, which made all the women laugh. Jared caught her eye and winked. She couldn't help but smile. He really was one hundred percent irresistible, one hundred percent of the time. Good thing she was marrying him. She'd never get enough.

After more drinks, cookies, and a rousing game of White Elephant with the most ridiculous gifts being traded back and forth, including a Scooby-Doo Chia plant, it was finally midnight and time for the real gifts. Emily couldn't wait to give hers to Jared. She had one for Vince too.

"Open mine first," Jared said to Emily.

She opened a small velvet box, expecting to see a ring. It was a key.

"It's the key to my house," he said. "I want you to move in with me. Like yesterday."

She laughed. "I will. Someone has to look after that shoulder."

"And a few other parts too," he said, waggling his eyebrows.

"Keep it down over there," Vince boomed.

"Here, open mine," she said, handing him a large flat box. "I got you one too, Vince." She handed Vince an identical box. "Open them at the same time."

Vince cocked a brow. "Must be pretty special if I get the same thing as Jare."

She nodded and smiled. Vince ripped his open first. Jared was a little slow, going one-handed. She finished the paper off for Jared so his surprise wouldn't be ruined.

Vince opened the box and peeled back the tissue paper to reveal a brand-new Captain Cuddle T-shirt with a big C sewn to the front. He promptly slammed the lid on the box. His neck and ears turned red.

"What is it?" Sophia asked.

Jared peeked at his own shirt with a big H sewn to the front.

"What's that?" Nico asked.

"It's our secret identity," Jared announced. "Vince has been dressing up like a porcupine from Mom's Huddle-Cuddle books to visit the pediatric oncology ward at the hospital."

The men laughed heartily. The women put an end to that with one sharp look.

"Cool," Luke said.

"Good work," Nico said.

"I'm a hedgehog from the book," Jared said. "I'll do it with you sometimes, Vince."

"Cool," Vince said. The tips of his ears turned an even brighter red. "Thanks, Emily. That was really…uh…"

"Thoughtful," Sophia supplied.

"Yeah," Vince said.

"You're welcome," Emily replied. She turned to Jared. "And I'm going to sew you a pointy little nose. I heard that's what hedgehogs look like."

Jared looked uncomfortable. "Ah. That's okay."

Now it was Emily's turn to tease. "What? Are you too cool to play a real hedgehog, Captain Huddle?"

"I'll do it," Jared said, rising to her challenge. "I'm just cool enough."

"Yeah, he is," Vince said. "He's our clutch player."

Emily kissed Jared. "He's my clutch player."

# EPILOGUE

Jared showed up with Vince in full costume for their New Year's Day hospital visit. His arm was still in a sling, so it helped to have his brother there to carry the books. At least that was what he told Vince. He could tell Vince just wanted an excuse to get back to being Captain Cuddle now that Sophia was feeling better.

Emily smiled at both of them, kissed them both on the cheek, and handed Jared the goody bag. "Go get them, Captains!"

"Hey, got room for two more?" a masculine voice boomed.

They turned. "Angel!" Jared exclaimed and then in a lower voice, "Julia."

"Are they together now?" Vince asked in a stage whisper.

"Shhh," Emily said.

Angel and Julia reached their side. Neither were dressed in any kind of costume.

"When I told Julia about your work here," Angel said, "she wanted to get involved."

"It's one of my New Year's resolutions," Julia explained. "Getting more involved in things."

Angel met her eyes with a searching look, and she quickly turned away.

"So, um, what can we do?" Julia asked.

"You could work the ward in the opposite direction and do some coloring with them," Emily offered. "The art therapist has been off for the holidays. Let me get the supplies."

She went to the closet and retrieved some paper and a bucket of crayons. "She often starts with a prompt to get them drawing, but also expressing themselves. Like, draw what family looks like or draw your favorite day."

Angel spoke up, never taking his eyes off Julia. "Since it's New Year's, we could try…draw a new beginning."

"That sounds like a good idea," Julia said softly.

Jared, Vince, and Emily gave each other knowing looks and then stumbled over each other to agree.

"Fantastic!" Jared said at the same time as Emily said, "Absolutely!"

"Get in there and get 'er done!" Vince boomed.

Everyone stopped to stare at him.

"What?" Vince asked.

Jared shook his head, making the quills bounce on his hat. "Come on. Leave them to it."

"That's what I was trying to do," Vince said.

The two brothers turned at the same time, their blue capes flying out behind them, and headed to the first room. Angel and Julia walked side by side, speaking in low tones. And Emily went back to work, knowing her patients would have a good New Year's Day thanks to a sweet porcupine, an adorable hedgehog, two best friends, and her.

Would you like to read a Bonus Epilogue for more Jared and Emily? Go to: http://www.kyliegilmore.com/clutchbonus

Don't miss the next book in the series, *A Tempting Friendship*, where Angel finally makes his move on his longtime friend Julia.

**Even Angels have their limits…**
Widow Julia Turner is finally ready to date again after five years of mourning her husband. She confides to her longtime friend Angel Marino that she's signed up for an online dating site and is shocked when it's Angel that shows up at her door on the night of her first date. And the look in his eye is anything but friendly.

Angel has secretly been in love with Julia since college, and after fulfilling his promise to his deceased best friend to watch over her these past years, he can't stand idly by and watch her date another man. It's time to unleash the sexy for a seduction that's been a *long* time coming.

Sign up for my newsletter and never miss a new release! https://www.kyliegilmore.com/newsletter

# ALSO BY KYLIE GILMORE

**Unleashed Romance <<steamy romcoms with dogs!**

Fetching (Book 1)

Dashing (Book 2)

Sporting (Book 3)

Toying (Book 4)

Blazing (Book 5)

Chasing (Book 6)

Daring (Book 7)

Leading (Book 8)

Racing (Book 9)

Loving (Book 10)

**The Clover Park Series <<brothers who put family first!**

The Opposite of Wild (Book 1)

Daisy Does It All (Book 2)

Bad Taste in Men (Book 3)

Kissing Santa (Book 4)

Restless Harmony (Book 5)

Not My Romeo (Book 6)

Rev Me Up (Book 7)

An Ambitious Engagement (Book 8)

Clutch Player (Book 9)

A Tempting Friendship (Book 10)

Clover Park Bride: Nico and Lily's Wedding

A Valentine's Day Gift (Book 11)

Maggie Meets Her Match (Book 12)

**The Clover Park Charmers series <<sweet and sexy charmers!**

Almost Over It (Book 1)

Almost Married (Book 2)

Almost Fate (Book 3)

Almost in Love (Book 4)

Almost Romance (Book 5)

Almost Hitched (Book 6)

**Happy Endings Book Club Series <<the Campbell family and a romance book club collide!**

Hidden Hollywood (Book 1)

Inviting Trouble (Book 2)

So Revealing (Book 3)

Formal Arrangement (Book 4)

Bad Boy Done Wrong (Book 5)

Mess With Me (Book 6)

Resisting Fate (Book 7)

Chance of Romance (Book 8)

Wicked Flirt (Book 9)

An Inconvenient Plan (Book 10)

A Happy Endings Wedding (Book 11)

**The Rourkes Series <<swoonworthy princes and kickass princesses!**

Royal Catch (Book 1)

Royal Hottie (Book 2)

Royal Darling (Book 3)

Royal Charmer (Book 4)

Royal Player (Book 5)

Royal Shark (Book 6)

Rogue Prince (Book 7)

Rogue Gentleman (Book 8)

Rogue Rascal (Book 9)

Rogue Angel (Book 10)

Rogue Devil (Book 11)

Rogue Beast (Book 12)

**Check out my website for the most up-to-date list of my books:**
**kyliegilmore.com/books**

# ABOUT THE AUTHOR

Kylie Gilmore is the *USA Today* bestselling author of over fifty humorous contemporary romances. Her series include Unleashed Romance, the Rourkes, the Happy Endings Book Club, Clover Park, and Clover Park Charmers. With more than three million downloads of her books, readers all over the world love escaping into her hilarious feel-good romances featuring strong bonds with family, friends, and community.

Kylie lives in New York with her family, a demanding cat, and a nutso dog. When she's not writing, reading hot romance, or dutifully taking notes at writing conferences, you can find her flexing her muscles all the way to the high cabinet for her secret chocolate stash.

Sign up for Kylie's Newsletter and get a FREE book! kyliegilmore.com/newsletter

For text alerts on Kylie's new releases, text KYLIE to the number (888) 707-3025. (US only)

For more fun stuff check out Kylie's website https://www.kyliegilmore.com.

Thanks for reading *Clutch Player*. I hope you enjoyed it. Would you like to know about new releases? You can sign up for my new release email list at https://www.kyliegilmore. com/newsletter. I promise not to clog your inbox! Only new release info, sales, and some fun giveaways.

I love to hear from readers! You can find me at:
    kyliegilmore.com
    Instagram.com/kyliegilmore
    Facebook.com/KylieGilmoreToo
    Twitter @KylieGilmoreToo

If you liked Jared and Emily's story, please leave a review on your favorite retailer's website or Goodreads. Thank you.